# THE HOOVER FILES
# AN 8MEN STORY

A NOVEL

MARCUS SMITH

Library of Congress

Valeir Publishing, Inc.
Landover Hills, Maryland

*I'm questioning the values and morals of the historians that write our text books.*

QUEZ

# THE LOOP

On April 11, 1971, "The Loop" in Chicago is quiet. It is the area that encompasses the city's home of the Federal Bureau of Investigation (FBI) and some popular restaurants and apartment buildings. The Easter holiday cleared out most bureau employees who may have been tempted to clock some extra hours. The only vehicle sitting on South Dearborn Street is a blue van with a young white man sitting in the driver's seat listening to a Bob Dylan record.

The FBI is housed on the 9th floor of the E.M. Dirksen Federal Building. The only people walking on the 9th floor appear to be the security staff and the janitorial workers. One of the young maids has been getting unwanted attention from one of the somewhat portly security guards.

"Your husband lets you come out on Easter Sunday," asks the guard.

"I don't have a husband, plus I have bills to pay," proclaims the maid as she bends over to dump some trash.

The maid's short skirt exposes her skimpy underwear and her shapely backside.

"Good Lord!" exclaims the excited security guard.

"Back here. That is the Chief's office?" inquires the maid.

"Umm," stammers the security guard as he is captivated by the maid's low-cut dress.

"I think I am supposed to clean in there too," hints the maid.

"Umm, I am not sure about that. Nobody goes back there," states the security guard nervously.

"I am pretty sure the Chief wants his office cleaned. I like private offices, and I get to do my dance," suggests the maid as she touches the guard's chest seductively.

The overly excited security guard fumbles through his keys to get the right key for the chief's office.

"I want to see this dance," remarks the guard as he finds the key. The guard places the key in the lock. Out of nowhere, the guard is hit in the head with a club. The guard falls lifelessly to the ground.

"Damn, you didn't have to hit him so hard," says the maid.

"Sandy, that is your fault. I should have hit him harder. He was making moves on my woman. Or maybe you like it?" questions Anthony Montgomery.

Former FBI agent Anthony Montgomery went underground after Raoul's warning about the plot to kill him. Montgomery stayed completely off the radar until early 1970, when he joined the Chicago Black Panther Party. Montgomery thought his previous FBI ties could help the Panthers find some answers about the apparent assassination of Panther Chicago Chief Fred Hampton. It was rumored that Hampton's murder was a hit ordered by the Chicago FBI. Over the last six months, Montgomery has partnered with a leftist organization named The Sunshine group to perform some political burglaries concentrating on finding information on corruption of government and political figures. Montgomery removes the painting behind the chief's desk. There is a combination safe behind the painting. He goes into his bag and pulls out a stethoscope and a small camera.

"What are you going to do with that?" asks the maid.

"I am going to listen to the tumbles of the lock to get the right number," claims Montgomery.

He spins the lock then rolls it 10 to the right, 1 left and then 44 right, then the safe pops open.

"Jackpot!" exclaims an excited Montgomery. He pulls out several file folders. He finds a file labeled Hampton; Montgomery starts to snap pictures of the items in the Hampton file, then finds a diagram of Hampton's home. The diagrams illustrate the best entrance to enter. Montgomery feels very satisfied with the info he is able to extract. He is about to put the file back when he sees a file labeled "8MEN." He opens the file to find the names and pictures of the 8MEN including Richard Teed. Montgomery realizes it is the man he knew as Raoul. Montgomery snapped pictures of everything.

"I have to find that number for The Squirrel," utters Montgomery.

# X

The second annual Malcolm X Day was taking place in different Negro conclaves throughout the United States. But the Washington, D.C. remembrance is occurring on the hollowed out U Street. The U Street corridor was hit hard by the fires that occurred during the 1968 riots following Dr. King's assassination. The once bustling area dominated by Negro businesses was now dominated by charred rubble. One of the only businesses to survive the six-day riot was Ben's Chili Bowl. Ben's Chili Bowl is the site for the 2nd Annual Malcolm X Day activities in the capital city. The day's theme was to resist the government, as several speakers had taken to the stage to talk about racism and self-reliance. The orators talked about systematic prejudice in America but reiterated that Black people must build businesses and stay united. Anthony Montgomery listened to several of the speakers. Montgomery had a momentary vision of Dr. King and what could have been. He thought of all his great work and wondered how he would feel about where Black people were today. Montgomery is scheduled to meet with someone at 2 pm inside Ben's Chili Bowl. He looks at his watch, it reads 1:57 pm. Montgomery moves through the crowd. The destruction around Ben's didn't dampen its booming business. The business' survival had revered it to the community. People of different races were now coming to Ben's just to be able to say they have been to the Northwest Washington restaurant. Montgomery goes through the door of Ben's; he sees the bustling crowd. Montgomery is third in line to order. He goes into his pants pocket and pulls out a piece of paper with the instructions, "order a sausage sandwich with onions, ask for extra onions." Montgomery steps up to the counter and orders.

"Can I have a sausage sandwich with extra onions on it?" asks Montgomery.

"Are you sure you want extra onions?" challenges the cashier as Montgomery looks at the mounds of onions on the grill.

"Umm, yeah," replies Montgomery.

"I hope you not meeting anybody, your breath is going to be tart," states the cashier.

The cashier puts in his order. Montgomery looks around the restaurant. He sees a black man waving him over. Montgomery points to himself to make sure the man is talking to him. The Black man nods his head. Montgomery carefully walks over to the man. Not knowing if he is being set up, Montgomery scans the room.

"Hello, my name is Montgomery, and you are?" inquires Montgomery.

"My friends call me The Squirrel. Are you a friend?" probes The Squirrel.

"I hope so," mentions a cautious Montgomery.

The Squirrel motions for Montgomery to sit in his booth.

"So, you need to get in touch with a mutual friend of ours?" asks The Squirrel.

"Yes, I want to warn him about Hoover," whispers Montgomery.

"What about Hoover," demands The Squirrel.

"Hoover has a dossier on the 8MEN group," concedes Montgomery.

Montgomery pulls out a file folder, he passes the folder to The Squirrel. The file reads covert missions performed by the 8MEN. "The Korean Village extraction, JFK takedown, MLK neutralization, Bobby Kennedy '68, Black Messiahs.

"The Director is monitoring this group himself," discloses Montgomery.

"God damn Hoover," utters The Squirrel.

"Do you know what this means?" quizzes Montgomery.

"Not all of it," says The Squirrel.

"So, what can we do?" asks Montgomery.

"I am going to have to get in touch with Teed. He…we are being set up," admits The Squirrel.

# MR. CARTER

CIA Director Wesley Carter has taken on much of the responsibility of the foreign intelligence portfolio since President Nixon's election in 1968. Carter has been pushed out of domestic intelligence by an overly paranoid FBI Director, J. Edgar Hoover. Carter was a bit perturbed by Hoover's exclusion of him into Domestic Affairs, but the Director has his reasons. Hoover was trying to keep his Cointelpro initiative close to the vest. Hoover knew that Carter was aware of the FBI's surveillance of Negro leaders because of their cooperation with regards to Martin Luther King, but he didn't want anyone outside of his immediate circle to know how far reaching the Cointelpro program really was. The agency's participation in the neutralization of Negro leaders could definitely get him and his top brass thrown in jail. Carter had his own issues keeping up with the Korean Peninsula and the bubbling problems of radical terrorism in the Middle East. Ever since the Arab countries' resounding defeat at the hands of the Israeli army, small Muslim radical groups have been performing small terrorist acts throughout the Middle East. Many of the acts were against Israeli owned assets, but recently there have been several acts against American and British owned assets over the last couple of months. Director Carter has become more concerned recently, one of his operatives sent an obscure article from an Egyptian newspaper. The article was on the emergence of the radical group the Muslim Brotherhood. An admitted bomber said, "We cannot beat the Israelites, the Americans or the British without militaries. We can only terrorize them with our unpredictability and withhold and overcharge for our natural resources. Carter knew that this disturbance would affect Americans and American interest abroad, so he'd better keep tabs on the area.

Director Carter is walking down the hall toward his office after a Middle East briefing in a nearby conference room. The director's secretary is on the phone as the director swiftly walks by.

"Director Carter," announces the secretary as she tries to catch him before he enters the office.

Director Carter enters his office to find The Squirrel sitting on a couch. The Director scoffs at The Squirrel's presence. The Director walks over to his desk and pulls out a cigarette.

"The Squirrel, correct?" states Carter.

The Squirrel gives the Director a dismissive look.

"You know who the hell I am. I am one of the people who could have started a shit storm after your little jungle party in 50," discloses The Squirrel.

"Mr. Squirrel, of course, I remember you. You were the greatest scout the army has ever seen," expresses a complimentary Carter.

"Damn good gun as well," replies The Squirrel.

The men shake hands, then sit down.

"I'll take it this is not a social call," queries Carter.

"No, you …we have a problem," hints The Squirrel as he pulls out a copy of the stolen FBI file.

"My name is in here and so are a lot of heavy hitters. You, Senator Capers, Cecil Thomas, Maximillion Love, Valerius Torrantio. You guys put together a hell of a group," alleges The Squirrel.

The obvious displeasure is evident on Director Carter's face.

"Thank you for bringing this to me," recites Carter.

"So, what do you want to do?" asks The Squirrel.

"I need to meet with my partners. I will let you know after I meet with them," declares Carter.

# OLD FRIENDS

The 8MEN have significantly prospered since the end of the Johnson administration. The growing Vietnam War has yielded each of the 8MEN a small fortune. The proceeds have allowed the group to invest in different businesses and reinvest in their own individual businesses.

Director Carter has decided to convene a meeting of the partners to discuss some long overdue loose ends that Carter felt should be tied up. The 8MEN have not seen each other in well over a year. The last few times they got together were more social than relevant to 8MEN matters. Director Carter walks into the room where the group are sitting. Carter is contemplating how he will broach the conversation of Hoover's betrayal. He sinks into his chair as he is still unsure how to start the discussion.

"Gentlemen, let's begin," suggests Carter.

"Shouldn't we wait for Edgar?" requests Murray Smith.

Carter scoffs before answering, "Hoover will not be meeting with us. He is the reason I called this meeting," he said.

"What has he done?" asks Thomas.

"He hasn't done anything, yet," alleges Carter.

"Yet?" chimes Maximillian Love.

"Carter just tell us," said Murray Smith.

Carter pulls out packets of paper. He passes the reports out to the 8MEN. The group flipped hastily through the documents. Carter pours himself a drink in anticipation of the questions that will undoubtedly arise after the 8MEN read the packets.

"Carter, what the hell is this?" probes Murray Smith.

"Please keep reading," responds Carter.

"Why the hell are there files about what we have done? It has our names, our wives' and children's names, addresses. Mistresses… Who does this belong to?" questions Cecil Thomas.

"I wanted you all to read the file. I know I could not do it justice. Director Hoover has been tracking our group before his membership and even after," reveals Carter.

"What could be the reason?" challenges Maximillian Love.

"Power and eventually blackmail," says Carter as he is interrupted by Valerius Torrantio's laughter.

"He is still mad over those fucking pictures from the 40s," claims Torrantio.

"Pictures, what pictures?" asks Thomas.

"Pictures of Hoover giving some guy a blowjob," divulges a laughing Torrantio.

Several of the 8MEN swear in disgust.

"I heard that before, but I figured it wasn't true. Hoover went after the gays with no mercy," mentions Thomas.

"It is true. I have seen the pictures. Had his face in the guy's cock," chuckles Torrantio.

"Fucking hypocrite," states Cecil Thomas.

"So now what?" asks Murray Smith.

"It is simple. Hoover must go. This is treacherous and pretty fucking ingenious. But again, he has got to go." says Torrantio as he stands up.

"Ok, knock him off, assassination style," said Carter.

"Don't know if we can do this one. Hoover is a bit insulated, plus he has these," says Murray Smith.

"Are we in agreement that he must go?" asks Carter.

The 8MEN stand in unison and say, "YES."

# THE DATE

Richard Teed and Danya Franck have been working undercover in the Middle East since they left the U.S. in 1968. Israel has been suffering many terrorist acts in the name of revenge for the Arab defeat during the Six-Day War in 1967. The Arab countries knew that Israel had a far more superior military to all the Arab countries combined. The politicians from the Arab countries decided to capitulate and end their outward desires to destroy the Jewish homeland. Once the Arab countries' politicians moved away from warring with Israel, the Muslim zealots stepped into the vacuum of hate. The zealots were not going to allow the Jews and by extension the Western powers to expel the Arabs and allow the Jews to occupy their holy land.

Richard Teed and Danya Franck are taking in the sites of Midtown Damascus. Teed and Danya sit in a quaint café looking out onto Straight Street, a main thoroughfare in the city. If one didn't know better, they would think Teed and Danya were in love. The couple is playing the part, and they are sitting in a booth together feeding each other finger sandwiches and sipping from the same Coca-Cola bottle. All the while they are staking out the restaurant across the street.

"I can't believe this is work," hints a smitten Danya.

"I love being with you also," replies Teed.

The romantic supper is interrupted when three limousines pull up to an elegant restaurant across the street from the café Danya and Teed are sitting in. Several men get out and rush to the middle limousine's back passenger door. All of the men are brandishing heavy artillery. Teed and Danya caught a tip that the Wajabaat restaurant played host to a monthly meeting of the Muslim Brotherhood. It was believed the Muslim Brotherhood was helping with logistical intelligence for some recent attacks, but it was well known that the organization was short on money. There was no way they could have pulled off some of the more recent episodes without help. Danya and Teed both gasp when Wafai Rashad emerges from the back of the limousine.

"I thought he was dead!" exclaims Teed.

"Roaches are hard to kill. You must squash them," expresses an enraged Danya.

"He is in the brotherhood," inquires Teed.

"Probably, but even worse, he is financing them. And his tentacles reach out to other powerful Muslim groups. This is not good…This is not good at all," said a distraught Danya.

# TERROR

The geopolitics of the Middle East have been complex at best since the beginning of the Six-Day War. The Arab countries have been stymied at every turn. Israel with help from its Western allies: France, England and the United States, have beat down the Arab countries attacks. The push back has forced some countries to recognize Israel so that there would be no reprisals. The lack of forceful talk about the destruction of Israel from the Arab countries has created a power vacuum. Several extremist groups have decided to pool their resources. Chief among the groups, the Muslim Brotherhood has invited members of the new radical group Black September to meet to brainstorm about how they can partner together on some terrorist attacks. The group adopted the moniker from the Black September conflict that occurred when Jordanian King Hussein cracked down on Palestinian fighters attempting a coup of his kingdom. The groups have decided that a frontal attack would not bare fruit but a more strategic attack on Israel and the West's soft targets may bring attention to the plight of the Palestinians. The coming together of the Muslim Brotherhood and Black September is an important development in the radical extremist movement, but the introduction of Wafai Rashad would prove to be more consequential. The groups have been meeting in a back room for hours arguing about how to make Israel pay for their aggressions against the Palestinians. Rashad has been sitting back for hours observing the short-sighted arguments between the groups. They bounce ideas off each other like destroying historic synagogues or prominent Israeli businesses in Jerusalem or Tel Aviv.

"You have nothing to add?" asks Amir Hakim, the head of the Muslim Brotherhood.

Wafai Rashad gives a slight chuckle as he puts out his cigar.

"Gentlemen, we are arguing with each other about how we make Israel pay. Israel is not our real enemy.

They are nothing but the lap dogs for the West. Sure, we destroy a synagogue or a business in Israel, that may make us feel good for a day or two. We have bombed their cafes, blown up their synagogues and destroyed some very prominent Jewish businesses. All we have gotten from that is being branded as savages and demonic. We have not told our narrative. But if we truly want to strike at the hearts of our oppressors, we must attack the comfort of the West. We must strike in a spectacular fashion," states Wafai. "What do you suggest?" requests Amir Hakim. Wafai Rashad is amused by his fiendish thoughts as he leans in to give his sentiments.

# UNWANTED GUESTS

Teed and Danya pull up to their apartment hideaway in Quneitra after driving for a little over an hour in complete silence. The couple pulls into a parking space in view of their apartment.

"We have to get a sanctioned kill order for Wafai. Hopefully, we will get it soon. Who knows how long we have until the next attack," says Danya.

"So, you are sure he is behind all the attacks?" asks Teed.

"Absolutely, I would bet my life on it," responds a confident Danya.

Teed looks at his second-floor apartment window. He notices the wind has moved the window curtain. Teed immediately looks around and pulls out his gun.

"What's wrong?" inquires a concerned Danya.

"I didn't leave that window open. You didn't leave the window open, did you?" requests a stern Teed.

"No," responds Danya.

"Maybe we have a little company," hints Teed.

Teed and Danya survey their immediate surroundings making sure nobody was going to surprise them as they exited the car. Teed and Danya exit the vehicle and walk toward the rear of the apartment building. The couple sneak up the rear entrance of the building. Danya pulls a 22-caliber pistol from her leg holster underneath her dainty unassuming dress before climbing the staircase. Danya and Teed carefully open the staircase door to the second floor. The couple gingerly walk down the hall toward their apartment. Danya and Teed are startled when an older woman comes out of her apartment. The woman is unaware of the danger she was in as she passes by Teed and Danya. Thinking they may be over-reading, the duo holster their weapons as they approach their apartment. Still cautious, Danya and Teed open, then step away from the door in case someone is waiting to shoot them as they entered. Danya and Teed peak around the corner to see if the coast is clear. In the absence of seeing anyone, they both enter the apartment. As Danya and Teed enter the apartment's living room area, they see a black man in his late 40's sitting in Teed's tweed reclining chair.

"I thought you two may be on vacation or something," asserts The Squirrel with a chuckle.

"Oh great, The Squirrel is here," utters Danya as she walks into the kitchen to put her purse down.

Teed walks over to The Squirrel and hugs him.

"Don't worry about her. This is a hell of a surprise," remarks Teed.

"So why are you here?" questions a precautious Danya.

"So glad to see you too, Miss Danya," responds The Squirrel.

"Glad to see you, but really why are you here?" asks Teed.

"Carter asked me to bring you back to the States," replies The Squirrel.

"We are tracking some terrorists. We don't have time for Director Carter's little games," pushes back Danya.

"It's actually a pretty important mission," the Squirrel declares.

"There is some important business you must tend to back in the states," suggests The Squirrel.

"What can be more important than shutting down terrorists?" challenges Danya.

"The exposure of the 8MEN," reveals The Squirrel.

Both Teed and Danya have a look of shock on their faces.

"Exposure by who?" inquires Teed.

"Hoover," implies The Squirrel.

"Why would Hoover expose the 8MEN. He is a part of the 8MEN, no?" asks Danya.

"Hey, looking at the information, the FBI has been tracking the group as well as us three for years. Carter and the whole group are pretty pissed," mentions The Squirrel.

"So now what?" asks Teed.

Danya proclaims, "We go back to America and kill HOOVER!!!!"

"Man, she is cute but scary at the same time," says The Squirrel as Danya leaves the room.

# REQUIEM

John Edgar Hoover, better known as J. Edgar Hoover, has been the most powerful man in the world since his ascension to the FBI's top chair in 1929. Four decades later, Hoover continues to be the preeminent law enforcement officer in the world. Still, recent public reports claim Hoover has been using government resources to spy on Americans and even commission the death of those considered subversive. After stolen FBI files were sent to media outlets, Hoover started to hear murmurs of a possible forced retirement or even criminal charges against him. Hoover's paranoid view of law enforcement was coming to light. The discovery of the FBI's Cointelpro program frightened many within and outside of the government. And the possible direct sanctioned assassination of Black Panther Fred Hampton seemed too much to stomach.

The evening of May 1st, 1972, ended like many evenings over the last month for FBI Director Hoover. With Hoover scouring local newspapers and national tabloids for his impending demise, he has been paying particular attention to the Washington Post and New York Times' front and editorial pages to see if there was any public sentiment toward his possible forced retirement. Hoover's driver pulls up to his Northwest Washington residence.

"Director, we are here," announces the driver.

Director Hoover looks up to find that he has arrived at his home. The Director gives the driver a half-smile and exits the vehicle. Hoover walks into his empty house with a resounding thud of his front door. After going through his mail, the Director walks upstairs. Hoover walks into his bedroom, sitting in his loveseat is Richard Teed.

"A ghost from my past," alleges a calm Hoover.

"Mr. Director," greets Teed.

"You could have made an appointment at my office," suggests Hoover.

"Not sure we want to talk about this in your office, Director Hoover," replies Teed.

"Oh," asserts Hoover as he plops down on his couch.

"Why is my name in a file that the FBI is keeping with your blessing? The files connect Danya and me to the King and Kennedy murders," claims Teed.

Hoover scoffs, "not only you and Ms. Franck but all of the 8MEN and their families. You all made too much money without me. I watched over the decades while the 8MEN made absurd amounts of money. Most by scheming and cheating the American people and calling it good business."

Teed responded, "Are you kidding me? You are concerned with the American people being cheated. You spy on their leaders, and those you can't leverage you kill," banters Teed with a certain venom.

Hoover starts to laugh, "That sounds like a man who has a guilty conscious," he added.

"Why the dossier on all of us?" questions Teed.

"Mr. Teed, we are all in the information business. I needed to know your information as well as the group's, in case I needed the proper leverage one day," admits Hoover.

"That wasn't needed," alleges Teed.

"Easy for you to say. There were some compromising pictures of me many years ago. Some of the men in this group controlled me with those pictures," remarks a reflective Hoover.

Teed feels pity for the aged Bureaucrat. He thought the decades of Hoover trying to keep his secret could have caused a major incident. As Teed is feeling some sort of pity for Hoover, Director Carter and Danya Franck walk in.

"Looks like the gang is all here," mocks Hoover.

The Squirrel walks in behind them.

"You are traveling with Negroes now, Carter, tisk...tisk," teases Hoover.

"He found your damaging info, Edgar," divulges Carter.

"We all have info. Are you trying to tell me you don't have info on these people, Carter. If you don't, you're a damn fool," verbalizes Hoover as he directs his comments toward Teed, Danya, and The Squirrel.

"Any information I have is not for blackmail," affirms Carter.

"That's what you say today. What happens the day they don't agree with you and become a threat? Then you will pull out your information to get them in line or you will simply kill them," proclaims Hoover. Danya, Teed, and The Squirrel look at each other like Hoover may be speaking prophetically about their future.

Where is your information? Do these young people have it. Or is the collection of information all one way?" snickers Hoover.

"Edgar, who has seen this info?" queries Carter.

"No one, but the President wants it. He knows your group exists. I have kept him at a distance, but Nixon is coming for it. I think he is waiting for my death to go through my papers. So, I guess you need to keep me alive," declares Hoover.

Carter stares deep into Hoover's eyes and addresses him.

"Edgar, you played this all wrong. Your important papers are here. We will get all the papers tonight," concedes Carter as Teed and The Squirrel restrain Hoover.

"What are you doing?" asks a struggling Hoover.

Danya pulls out a syringe.

"Mr. Hoover, this is going to make you very sleepy," utters Danya.

"A permanent sleep, goodbye Edgar," announces Carter as he walks out.

Hoover fades off into a deep sleep. His eyes roll back into his head as his body goes limp.

"Now what?" inquires Teed.

"In the morning, Hoover's maid or butler will discover his lifeless body. He will have died of a massive heart attack," says Carter matter of factly as he walks out of the room.

"That is a bad dude," remarks The Squirrel as he and Teed watch Carter leave.

# WIDOWER

Clyde Tolson has been the Associate Director of the FBI since the early 1930s. Tolson's fortunes have been closely tied to J. Edgar Hoover's power. It's been long-rumored Hoover and Tolson have been romantically linked since Tolson's entrance into the agency. Hoover has always credited Tolson with the strict discipline and impeccable demeanor of the bureau's agents.

Shortly after midnight, there is a knock on Clyde Tolson's apartment door. Tolson gets out of bed; he walks over to the door. Tolson looks through the peephole. He doesn't recognize the people on the other side of the door.

"Yes, who is it?" asks a half-asleep Tolson.

"Wesley Carter."

Tolson is snapped out of sleepiness.

"Wesley, how can I help you?" inquires a nervous Tolson.

Tolson and Carter have known each other for years at a distance. They have met several times at holiday parties, and both have briefly talked at a few inaugurations over the years. But they weren't close enough for Carter to ring his doorbell after midnight.

"Clyde, we need to talk. It is about Edgar," remarks Carter.

Tolson is not an experienced field agent, but his agent nervousness is kicking in.

"Where is Edgar?" questions Tolson.

"Clyde, we need to talk. Edgar is gone," says Carter.

Whatever nervousness Tolson felt was now replaced by emptiness. He begins to open the door. Tolson stands at the partially opened door with a single tear rolling down his cheek.

"Clyde, I am sorry for your loss. May, I come in?" asks Carter.

Tolson steps to the side and invites Carter in.

"How, what happened to Edgar," asks a grief-stricken Tolson.

"May I sit?" requests Carter.

Carter walks over to the dining room table and sits down.

"Clyde, Edgar died of a heart attack. He told me to come to you to get the other private files. He knew that once the President discovered that he was dead, they would come for all the files. Can you please get those files?" requests Carter with no regard for Tolson's loss.

Tolson gets up to get the files. As he starts to walk away, an angry Tolson turns toward Carter, pointing a .38 revolver at him.

"Let's try this again. What the hell happened to Edgar?" demands a defiant Tolson.

Understanding the jig is up, Carter decides to level with Tolson.

"You were always smart, Clyde," suggests a calculating Carter.

"Don't you patronize me; I want the whole truth," replies an angry Tolson.

"Ok. We poisoned Edgar. We made it look like he had a heart attack," reveals Carter.

"Why?" inquires a weeping Tolson.

"He had a number of files that could ruin all our members. Edgar was looking to blackmail the group," divulges Carter.

"He was only doing it to ensure none of you would release the pictures," says Tolson.

"Pretty soon, the powers that be were going to come for him. All the Cointelpro, the Hampton Murder and countless other things. Clyde, his days were numbered. He didn't have much to bargain with. Edgar would have given us up. Clyde, give me the files so that this can be done," demands Carter. "You thought you were going to come here, and I was just going to give you Edgar's insurance policy? It is supposed to be that easy?" asks Tolson.

"Yes, it is. Clyde, you are smart. Edgar left you everything. You will get that file, and I am going to give you this," Carter hands Tolson a folder. The folder has the long-rumored pictures of Tolson and Hoover in a compromised position.

"So now you are going to blackmail me?" challenged an embarrassed Tolson.

"No, this is a peace offering. There are no more. These are yours. This is it," reveals Carter.

Tolson thinks long and hard about Carter's offer.

"Stay here. I will get it," affirms Tolson as he leaves the room to get Carter the file.

# YESTERYEAR

The 8MEN have amassed deep and consequential secrets over the past four decades. So, the possibility of J. Edgar Hoover blackmailing the group could not stand. Hoover was under pressure to resign, but the old G-Man said to many privately, "Let the son of a bitches come for me. I have information on everyone. I am the keeper of America's greatest secrets. Those that know I know their secrets better help to keep me alive and out of jail." Director Carter left Clyde Tolson's swanky Upper Northwest D.C. neighborhood feeling relieved and curious. Carter knew that Hoover would never leave his most sensitive files at his home. He knew that was where everyone would start looking. The file is a who's who of powerful people. Understanding Hoover, Carter knew that the most sensitive information would be left with Clyde Tolson. And Carter's gut proved to be spot on. Carter ferociously flips through the file; he notices information on Martin Luther King. Carter stops to read the information on King. Hoover writes that "King is a tomcat. He portrays himself as a man of the cloth, but he is nothing but a sexual beast. He and his co-conspirators have sex parties. They are all hypocrites." Carter thumbs through more of the file, he stops at the "Red Scare." The information centers on Hoover's fear of Communism. Hoover was convinced that any hint of Communism needed to be snuffed out. He believed Hollywood and the Civil Rights movement were being influenced by the Communism movement. Hoover believes McCarthy has been an albatross to the Anti-Communist movement. Although he understands McCarthy's disdain, he didn't agree with his methods. Carter flips to information with his name front and center. "Wesley Carter is an up-and-coming bureaucrat. He is smart, a true tactician. He sees things several steps ahead. Hope he doesn't waste his talent and become a politician. Carter has started to consort with some unsavory characters, not sure if he is making them assets or if he is monetizing his position. Carter has become a major player in the intelligence community, he has become the point person for the Latin country assassinations. Carter has been using some Negro officers in these operations, guessing he wants some plausible deniability." Carter looked at the file with a strange sense of pride. The most famous law enforcement officer ever touted that Carter helped stabilize the United States after World War II. But as Carter continued to read, he noticed the tone of the notes began to change. "Carter has become friends with Hampton Capers. Worst thing he could have done. Capers is a hypocrite. He portrays himself as a son of the south, but he is nigger-lover. He has a half-breed child with a former maid. HYPOCRISY!!!

Carter commissioned a covert mission into Korea with Capers' backing. The mission was veiled as a peacekeeping mission to find some missing American POWs. The mission was to find a biological weapon created by the Nazis. The weapon is an autoimmune virus designed to kill the host after exchange of body fluids. Carter, Capers and several other men have formed a somewhat secret group, not sure what they are up to." Carter takes a deep breath uttering, "Damn you Edgar."

# MOURNING

On May 3rd, 1972, Americans awaken to the news that J. Edgar Hoover died of an apparent heart attack overnight. All the local news channels are broadcasting stories about Hoover. Many of the people interviewed on TV are in shock. Even though many had grown to despise Hoover, they couldn't remember a time without him. Hoover's tenure spanned six U.S. Presidents. Many of the Presidents and members of Congress feared Hoover's ability to find out politicians' darkest secrets and then leverage those secrets against them. It was those secrets that sealed Hoover's fate.

Teed and Danya are staying in room 414 of the luxurious Watergate Hotel in Northwest Washington, D.C. The pair are combing through years of Hoover's files. Hoover kept files on every American he found subversive and those he found a threat to him. He held a file he called "Presidential Affairs." Teed reads in "Presidential Affairs" accounts of Franklin Roosevelt's extramarital affairs and First Lady Eleanor Roosevelt's long-standing liaisons. "Presidential Affairs" speaks of several presidents' sexual trysts, but much of the file is dedicated to President Kennedy. The files outline JFK's sexual exploits before and after his presidential election. Hoover's file seemed to explore Kennedy's mistresses' connection to the mob and liberal-leaning Hollywood. It appears from the file that Hoover presented his findings to President Kennedy before many of the Cointelpro wiretaps were signed off on.

"This guy was a piece of work," suggests a stunned Teed as he continues to go through the files.

Danya is reading the file labeled "8MEN." The file begins with a brief history of Hampton Capers. The file labels Capers, the co-founder of the 8MEN. Capers was credited with bringing the shadowy group's government ties and its financial resources. Wesley Carter is labeled as the other co-founder. Carter is described as the brain trust of the 8MEN and the executioner of necessary business. The file describes individual missions the 8MEN spearheaded, including the fixing of the 1960 presidential election, the Dimona nuclear plant, the Kennedy and MLK assassinations, and the Osage Tribe murders.

"What is this?" inquires a dumbfounded Danya.

Danya had some knowledge of most of the 8MEN's endeavors, but the Osage Tribe murders were foreign. Danya looked through a box of files. She finds the file labeled "Osage Tribe murders," she begins to read.

"What the hell does Bowen have to do with this?" Danya asks herself rhetorically.

# DICK

The re-election campaign for President Richard Milhous Nixon was running along smoothly in July of '72. The President had on-going issues with the Vietnam War and the country's racial strife, but all-in-all, the President was doing very well in the polls. The Washington Sun was running polls that had Nixon leading Democratic challenger George McGovern by 20 points in certain polls. Much of America felt good about Nixon. He appeared to be tough on crime and seemed to be steering America in the right direction.

President Nixon has summoned Director Carter to the Oval office. Carter and the President have not spoken at length since the death of J. Edgar Hoover. The President has had some people looking through papers found at Hoover's office and his home. The President knows there had to be other files. Nixon knew Hoover kept records on most public officials, including himself, but files Nixon expected to turn up have not. The President knew Carter and Hoover had become fast friends. Carter walks into the oval office.

"Mr. President," says Carter as he extends his hand to the President.

"Thank you for coming by; please have a seat," says the President.

The President sits down in his chair, looking for a conversation starter.

"So…so, wasn't that a darn shame about Edgar," utters an uncomfortable Nixon.

"Yeah, he was a good man," rebuts Carter.

"Hoover had a lot of files. We found a lot after his death, but there seemed to be several files missing. I don't have to tell you Hoover kept a file on every politician and powerful person in the U.S.," alleges the President.

"Mr. President, I will keep an eye out for any missing files," conveys Carter.

Nixon walks over to the patio door that looks out onto the rose garden.

"Director Carter, I hope we can come to some sort of understanding. Hoover told me about your 8MEN group. I am pretty sure your group was all through Hoover's files. We couldn't find anything about your group, and we couldn't find anything about me. I am hoping that any file about me shows up. I would hate to see you and your people subjected to government hearings into Jack and Bobby Kennedy and Reverend King's assassinations. Not to mention the ridiculous amounts of money you and your cronies have made on the Vietnam War," remarks President Nixon.

"Mr. President are you blackmailing me?" challenges Carter.

"Call it what you want. I want some information. I am pretty sure you have what I am looking for. Give me that info, and you never have to worry about anything from me. But if you get nothing, I will come for you and your band of riffraff," pronounces an intense President Nixon.

# HUDDLE

President Nixon's demand to get the files Director Carter took from J. Edgar Hoover's house has shaken the 8MEN. The 8MEN have enjoyed a certain amount of anonymity. No one had made the connection between the group and their collective goals. If Carter asked for some information that helps Valerius Torrantio's mob associates, no one has been the wiser, but when the President of the United States starts asking questions and implies, he will make things uncomfortable, it makes everyone nervous.

"So do we give Nixon the file?" asks Carter.

"If it keeps the President off our asses, give him the goddam file," responds Lance Bowen.

"I'm not sure it is that easy. Hoover had some info that makes Nixon very nervous," suggests Carter.

"Did you look at it all? Can we use it to our advantage?" inquires Valerius Torrantio.

"The file is concise but incomplete. It mentions plumbers and the Watergate," replies Teed.

The group is bewildered.

"Give him that bullshit. Don't take on the President over that," says Valerius.

"There is more to this, but Valerius, you are right. We will give this file to the President. Murray, could you put any of your investigative reporters on this story? Make sure they slow walk this. You can't be connected. Nixon is watching us," declares Carter.

"I have somebody in mind for this kind of story," claims Murray Smith.

"Is everybody in agreement?" Carter queries the group.

The group agrees in unison.

"That being said, let's adjourn," says Carter.

The group of 8MEN start to move away from the table. Teed moves around the table toward Lance Bowen.

"Mr. Bowen, you have a moment," asks Teed.

"Sure," responds Bowen.

Teed looks around the room to see if anyone is paying attention. I found information in Hoover's file about the Osage Indian Tribe murders. It seemed to be linking your grandfather to the murders," Teed divulged.

Instantly, rage overcomes Lance Bowen. His face shows his displeasure in Teed's assertion. But Bowen lessens the irritation before speaking.

"Mr. Teed, every family has secrets. Sometimes, some misunderstandings gather traction after people die, not allowing them to set the record straight or give some type of context. I have heard those rumors before, myself. My grandfather and my father were very complicated men. Hell, they were hard to get along with, but murderers they were not," claims Bowen.

Teed listens to Bowen's inadequate explanation and assumes what he read about the Bowen family is true.

"Here is the file in its entirety. As far as I know, this is the only copy," says Teed as he hands the file to Bowen.

The group starts to file out of the meeting room.

"Carter, you got a moment," asks Torrantio

"Sure," responds Carter.

"Tell me something about Agnew," requests Torrantio.

"You mean, the Vice President? What do you want to know?" asks Carter.

"Is he a stand-up guy?" quizzes Torrantio.

"Don't know him. I cannot vouch for him," conveys Carter.

"Ok, I appreciate it," says Torrantio.

"Is everything alright?" asks Carter.

"A friend hasn't gotten a return on their investment. They are just watching the situation. Agnew just needs to do the right thing," Torrantio expresses.

# ZEALOTS

The royal family of Saudi Arabia is preparing for a royal wedding. Prince Abdul-Rahman Saud will be marrying his first cousin Alya Rashad. The Saudi royals, like royals before them, generally marry within their family. The thought has been the royals wanted their children with like people, and there was no more like people than your first cousin. The pre-marriage festivities have taken the male participants to the desert and mountainous area of Baluchistan, Pakistan. The groom's tradition in the House of Saud was to travel to Baluchistan to hunt the beautiful Taloor birds in preparation for their weddings.

The men of Saud have been hunting for hours, and they have killed many of the beautiful Taloor birds. They return from hunting in a convoy of jeeps with the carcasses of the colorful birds draped off their vehicles' back bumpers. The royal servants meet the returning convoy as they return to their secluded cottages. The gentlemen get out of their vehicles, happy about the day's conquest.

"Hello everyone, it seems you have had a good hunt," says Wafai Rashad.

The group gives a collective sigh as they realize Wafai is on the porch of the cottage. Several of his cousins pass him with a half hello. Wafai laughs it all off. His extra-curricular activities have made it difficult for anybody to associate with him. Several family members have been subjected to international investigations looking for links between their company's finances and Wafai's terrorists' activities. Al-Aziz Saud, the crown prince of the Saudi dynasty, is the eldest son of King Khalid Saudi Arabia. King Khalid's fourth-youngest son Fahd was Wafai and Alya's father, his niece and soon-to-be daughter-in-law. Al-Aziz and Wafai greet each other by kissing each other on the cheeks.

"So, Wafai, why are you here?" asks Al-Aziz.

"Like you, cousin, I am here to celebrate family," says Wafai.

"Doesn't work for me, why are you here?" rebuts Al-Aziz.

"To reconnect with my family and to reconnect my family to Allah," declares a passionate Wafai.

"Wafai, what are you talking about? We are all devout to Allah," counters Al-Aziz.

Wafai steps away to laugh.

"My dear cousin, we have allowed our wealth to make us the lap dogs for the infidels. Decades ago, they could have cared less about us. But now, they love us. We have made ourselves whores for their money, and they're overindulgences," asserts Wafai.

Al-Aziz charges Wafai and lifts him by his coat lapels.

"You say we are not devout, and you call your family whores," Al-Aziz grills Wafai before releasing him.

"I am sorry for upsetting you, cousin," says a remorseful Wafai.

"Disrespect your family, and you name call us vile names because we will not join your jihad. We all see what you are trying to do. We want to live in peace. You want to fight an unwinnable war against the West. You have become a radical zealot. You have perverted the religion of our fathers," conveys Al-Aziz.

"I disagree. The way I see it, the very people you sell oil too, soil the lands of our religion," replies Wafai.

"Wafai, what do you want?" asks Al-Aziz.

"Cousin, I want the West to respect us. I want things to be fair to Arabs," says Wafai as he walks away.

# MASS DISTRACTION

Director Carter knew that he needed to put President Nixon's mind at ease. But Carter knew that the 8MEN were going to have to get some leverage on Nixon. Carter knew they were going to have to investigate what got the President so spooked. He decided to give Nixon a small amount of info from the mounds the 8MEN took from Hoover's home in order to pacify the President's fears. Carter decides to approach his extraction of information from Hoover's home as protecting the President and the country's interests.

Director Carter arrives at the Oval Office to a very warm reception from President Nixon.

"Director Carter, please come in." welcomes Nixon.

As Carter enters the Oval Office, he hands the President a manilla folder.

"Mr. President, we have a minimal amount of info.

The paperwork in the file mentions plumbers and the Watergate Hotel.

I have asked several of my contacts if they can make heads or tails of this information, and to this point, nobody knows what any of this means," discloses Director Carter.

The President is visibly relieved that Carter cannot make the connection between the plumbers and the Watergate.

"Carter, I appreciate you looking into this matter. But after I thought about it, it is probably for the best if we leave this the thing alone," responds Nixon.

"Are you sure, Mr. President? We can put some feelers out there," asks Carter.

"No," replies Nixon emphatically.

The President's reaction surprises Carter.

"I apologize. I don't want to waste your agency's valuable resources," comments the President.

"Ok, sir," says Carter as he gives a half-grin.

"I want to thank you, Carter for being loyal and being a great patriot," says Nixon.

"I appreciate that sir. I'm pretty sure you have a busy day, so I am going to go," says Carter as the men shake hands.

Carter walks to his awaiting car in the driveway of the White House. Murray Smith is in the car. Carter gets in the car smiling from ear to ear.

"So, how was the meeting?" asks Smith.

"He is surely hiding something," says Carter.

"What?" rebuts Smith.

"Whatever it is has got him paranoid," Carter added.

"Now what?" asks Smith.

"We must move very carefully, but I want you to leave breadcrumbs for others. Get a private investigator to connect the dots, then give the info to the FBI. They will surely find some things out. Also, give info to The Post, do not have The Sun report on any of this info. Again, we don't want our fingerprints on this info. Nixon will fuck himself in the end," suggests Carter.

# THE DNC

On Sunday June 18, 1972, The Washington Sun ran with the headline "5 Men Caught Breaking into the Dems National Office." The article goes on to report that an unnamed former CIA employee was arrested early Sunday morning. The article further explains that three of the burglars were men from Cuba. According to the police, it is believed that is not a simple robbery. The prowlers were well-dressed, and each had several hundreds of dollars in their wallets. Not to mention that electronic listening devices were seized in the arrest. On Monday June 19th, Director Wesley Carter is picking up The Washington Sun when his office phone rings.

"Hello," answers Carter. He checks his watch. "I can be there at 11am," says Carter.

Director Carter arrives at the White House at 10:50 am. He is quickly ushered into the Oval Office.

"He is in quite the mood," remarks the President's secretary as Carter enters the office.

The President is visibly agitated. He is on the phone with J. Edgar Hoover's replacement, Acting FBI Director L. Patrick Gray. Acting

Director Gray is briefing President Nixon on the Democratic National Committee's office break-in.

"Why is the FBI involved in this? Why not allow Metropolitan to investigate?" inquires Nixon.

Nixon is pacing back and forth while Gray explains why the FBI should investigate the burglary.

"I want your report to come to me and me alone. Do you understand me?" Nixon explains as he slams the phone.

There is awkward silence as Carter sits and watches the President fume with anger.


"Mr. President, I can come back if you need a few moments," says Carter as he creeps towards the office door.

"Carter, please stay," replies Nixon as if he just snapped out of a trance.

"How about I fix you a drink? What is your poison?" asks Nixon with a slight grin on his face.

"No thank you, sir," interjects Carter.

"Please have a seat," says Nixon

"Mr. President is everything alright?" asks a hesitant Carter.

"Everything will be," replies Nixon with a slight demented grin.

All of a sudden Carter had a very uneasy feeling.

"Sir, what can I do for you?" asks Carter.

"Answer a few questions for me. Do you know James McCord?" queries Nixon.

"I do, sir. He was a pretty good operative. Is he ok? asks Carter.

"He and several Cubans were arrested trying to break in at the DNC," says Nixon.

Carter is beginning to realize the gravity of the situation. He is wondering if the President is worried about McCord or is he afraid of the trail from McCord to himself.


"Never thought I'd ever miss Hoover. He would have handled this appropriately. I can't reason with that goddamn Gray, the power has gone to his head," responds Nixon.

"What won't he do," asks Carter as he listens intently to understand Nixon's direction.

"If the FBI looks too deep into this, it could turn into a mess," says Nixon.

"A mess sir?" asks Carter.

"But what if McCord couldn't be investigated because it could be a national security risk. You could talk to Gray and let him know that this investigation has stop," says a delusional President Nixon.

Carter can see that there is no reasoning with the President in his current state.

"Mr. President, I will talk to Gray. Hopefully, we can come to a meeting of the minds," says Carter as he tries to leave.

"Thank you very much Wesley. Don't let me down," says the President as Director Carter exits the Oval Office. Moments later, Carter gets into the car that is waiting for him outside of the West Wing. Carter gets into the back seat where Murray Smith has been waiting.

"So how did it go?" asks Smith.

"The DNC burglary has got him shook. The President is hiding something," says Carter as the car pulls off.

# THE TEXAN

Director Carter has always felt a debt of gratitude toward former President Lyndon Baines Johnson. Carter decided to inform and take the dossier Hoover prepared on him to President Johnson's ranch in Texas. Hoover and Johnson had a warm relationship as things go inside Washington, but Hoover documented Johnson's secrets as if they were lifelong enemies. Carter decided to burn most of the files recovered from Hoover's home but several files he took to the subjects. Notably, he took files to the widows of both Martin Luther King Jr. and Malcolm X. Carter visited them both and apologized for the invasion into their personal lives and expressed his admiration for both men's passion to make mankind better. However, Carter omitted that he played a vital part in the Civil Rights icons demise. President Johnson has stayed out of the public eye since the inauguration of Richard Nixon in January 1969. With the exception of a small contingent of secret service agents, President Johnson had left the bubble of the presidency back in Washington. Knowing that Director Carter was on his way to the house, President Johnson met Carter on his sprawling porch.

"Mr. President," says Carter.

"Wesley," responds President Johnson as they shake hands.

"No need for formality with me. We have been through too much together for that," comments President Johnson with a chuckle.

Carter hands President Johnson the dossier.

"What is this?" queries President Johnson.

"It is the information that Hoover had on you. He had them on all Washington insiders and on some big wigs in Hollywood," responds Carter.

President Johnson puts down the dossier without opening it.

"Ole, Edgar. Such a paranoid man. He believed he needed leverage on everyone because of his own deep-seated secrets," says an introspective President Johnson.

"You don't want to take a look?" asks Carter.

"No, I have done enough evil that surely has been documented. I've lived the best life I knew how. I am not going to debate the good and bad," remarks President Johnson in a reflective tone.

"Is that why you decided not to run in '68?" questions Carter.

President Johnson lets out a hardy laugh.

"No. I was terribly exhausted. With the weight of the world constantly on your shoulders, it is hard to rest. The constant chants from the protesters, I was just worn out. They accused me of killing our soldiers and murdering babies. Every man has his breaking point. I just thought the country needed a new direction; a new voice," concedes President Johnson.

"I thought you may have thought that Nixon would beat you," implies Carter.

"You never know, if I had the energy, Nixon wouldn't have stood a chance. I did a lot wrong, but I did do some good. Civil Rights was a really good thing. You know I was against it at first. But it was the right thing to do. There is a lot that many of us are going to have to answer for on judgement day," proclaims Johnson as tears stream from both his eyes.

Carter nods his head in the affirmative.

"Have you taken Nixon his file," asks Johnson.

"I did. He was searching for it," affirms Carter.

"I'm pretty sure that was an interesting read," suggests President Johnson.

"It was," states Carter as the two men share a chuckle.

"Wesley watch your back. Hoover was a known constant. There may be others far worse than him. Someone will try to fill the void. When you kill one snake, two more slither out," asserts President Johnson.

# THE PACT

The Hoover Files have greatly angered Fritz Kahn. There was no way Kahn was going to allow the death of his cousin J. Edgar Hoover go unavenged. His blood boils every time he thinks about how his cousin may have spent his final moments. Kahn is resolute to the destruction of the 8MEN. He wants to make the members of the Cabal suffer. Kahn is prepared to use his considerable resources to even the score with the 8MEN, but he wanted to reach out to someone equally bent on revenge. Several years ago, Wafai Rashad was thought to be dead as a result of a plane crash over Damascus. Luckily for Wafai, he missed the plane but never realized he was the intended target. He arrives at the swanky office of Fritz Khan. Wafai walks hesitantly up to Kahn's middle-aged secretary.

"I am here to see Mr. Kahn," announces Wafai.

"Go right in. He has been expecting you," replies the secretary.

Wafai walks through the office door nervously, not knowing what to expect.

"Mr. Rashad, please come in," utters Kahn.

"Are you Kahn?" inquires Wafai.

"I am Fritz Khan. But more importantly you want to know why you are here?" he replies.

Wafai shakes his head in the affirmative.

"We are kindred spirits. We have common enemies. A group of men and one woman have injured us both greatly and they must pay," declares Kahn.

"Injured, how were we injured? I don't even know you," recites Wafai.

"A week ago, I didn't know you existed either. I received an envelope from my cousin Edgy," reveals Kahn.

"I have never met anyone named Edgy," responds Wafai.

"Maybe you don't know him as Edgy. But the world knew him as J. Edgar Hoover," snaps Kahn.

"Whoa, I certainly know him," admits Wafai.

"My cousin kept a file on all the movers and shakers in the U.S. and some outside of the U.S. My cousin could probably be thought of as a bit paranoid. But he led the FBI for decades. He kept this country safe and free of Communism. And what do they do? Cast him out like he was yesterday's garbage. I need revenge to settle my soul," admits a nostalgic Kahn.

Wafai is wondering why he is here. "This all sounds pretty unnerving, but I didn't know your cousin," affirms Wafai.

"I know you are still wondering why you are here. Maybe this file can clear up some things for you?" discloses Kahn as he slides a file with Wafai's name on it.

"I hope it is good reading," says Kahn as Wafai starts to read his file.

"Who are these 8MEN?" questions Wafai as he looks up from the file.

# THE CAMEL JOCKEY

Wafai Rashad came to New York City not knowing that his entire life was about to change. Fritz Kahn gave Wafai a manilla folder with his entire life documented. The file chronicles Wafai's life from birth through Hoover's death. The file is filled with pertinent information about Wafai's extreme activities along with racists rants from Hoover about him and his culture. The file reads, "Wafai Rashad was born in Jeddah, Saudi Arabia in 1933. Wafai is the 3rd of 17 children born to Fahd Rashad. His father was a prince in the House of Saud. Fahd became an oil baron after attending Oxford University in England. 'He did quite well for a camel jockey,' comments Hoover in the margin of his notes. Wafai is visibly annoyed by the racist comment but continues to read. Wafai Rashad was educated in the states at Yale University. He double majored in industrial engineering and corporate finance development. Rashad earned no grade less than an A his entire collegiate career. In the margin, Hoover comments that Rashad came to the U.S. to be educated but ironically, he wanted to use what he learned to destroy us. Rashad was a typical college student until he was assaulted during his college graduation weekend. He and his girlfriend also of Arab descent were beaten up and mocked in a bar. The event set Rashad on a course to fight Western culture and its overt disrespect towards nonwhites.

The incident on his graduation weekend made Wafai re-examine his Muslim teachings. Up to that point, he believed that the overly accepting façade that America peddled to the world was true about all men being equal. He now knew that Americans and by extension Westerners were always going to look at him as an outsider. Upon arrival back to Saudi Arabia, Rashad began looking into the teachings of the Muslim Brotherhood. He quickly gained the trust and responsibility from the brotherhood's higher ups. Because of his background, Rashad showed members of the brotherhood how to create inexpensive explosives that would cause destruction with minimal instruction. The Muslim Brotherhood with his help started to perform small acts of defiance toward Western soft targets. The thought was the West had invaded the holy lands and it was now war. In 1970, Rashad suggested that the Muslim Brotherhood sabotage certain oil fields and extort others. He understands the West needs fossil fuels to power its massive factories and to heat its citizens' homes. He has learned that the Arab people cannot beat the West through force but with coordination the Arab people can most certainly make the West afraid.

# THE ENEMY

Fritz Kahn's disdain for the people he believed to be responsible for the death of his cousin J. Edgar Hoover was palpable. He wanted to destroy the group, but he wanted them all to suffer before he ultimately killed them all. Kahn knew strategically it was best to have an ally who would have just as much desire to see all the 8MEN dead. Wafai Rashad would be the perfect ally. His expertise and his rage would complement Kahn's plan. Kahn knew that if he showed Wafai the file Hoover compiled on the 8MEN he would certainly join him. Wafai is unaware of why Kahn would summon him, and he had no idea who the 8MEN were.

"I am supposed to know who these people are?" asks Wafai.

"Maybe you don't know them, but they know you. Please continue to read," requests Fritz Kahn.

Wafai begins to read Hoover's file. The genesis of the 8MEN began with the end of World War II. Senator Hampton Capers wanted the United States to take advantage of the global destruction that laid waste to every global power with the exception of the United States. Capers reached out to former OSS chief Wesley Carter to provide intelligence and the muscle that would eventually be needed. These men have set out to monetize the pain the world was going through. The 8MEN pushed for infrastructure deals or military protection in countries that were friendly to bribes that made them small fortunes. In an effort to take full advantage of any money that could be made, the 8MEN brought in certain Americans. The group brought in Syndicate Boss, Valerius Torrantio to provide muscle for nongovernmental actions and to access off the books funding. Next the group brought in media mogul Murray Smith, Smith has used his position to hide news stories or to change the narrative as needed. Steadman Industries CEO, Cecil Thomas provided the 8MEN its greatest revenue stream with selling munitions to everyone. Thomas sold to both sides of the Arab/ Israeli conflicts. Thomas sold weapons to Wafai years ago but now realizing he also sold to his enemies greatly angered him.

"Greedy white men. What's new?" declares Wafai as he slides the folder back to Kahn.

"Did you see your name in this file?" challenges a sarcastic Kahn.

"My name for what?" asks Wafai.

"There was a contract on your life," discloses Kahn as he slides the file back to Wafai.

Wafai hastily flips through the pages to the name Danya Franck. The file reads Mossad agent Danya Franck has been in league with the 8MEN since the early 1950s. Ms. Franck carried out a contract to eliminate Muslim Brotherhood chief Wafai Rashad. Unbeknownst to Ms. Franck, Wafai Rashad was not on the plane that he was scheduled to be on. But his wife and two sons were not as lucky, they all perished in the crash. The pain of the day rushed back to the still heartbroken Wafai Rashad.

"What do I need to do?" demands Wafai as tears stream from his eyes.

# THE HUNT

The Watergate break-in was so dangerous to the Nixon administration because it brought together operatives from many of the most covert operations over the past two decades. E. Howard Hunt was with the CIA for 20 years before he left to become a security consultant for the Nixon administration. Hunt was a living time capsule for the American clandestine community. He participated or was consulted on every high value covert mission since 1949. The imprisonment of Hunt did not just scare the Nixon administration but all that had been in the intelligence community over last half century. It was rumored that Hunt was instrumental in several coups in Central America and Iran. He gave tactical instruction to Cuban exiles involved in the Bay of Pigs operation, and he provided military resources for the murders of President Kennedy and Martin Luther King. Washington insiders on both sides of the isle have been nervous since the arrest of Hunt. Much like Carter, Watergate itself was not the issue that worried so many. It was the endless number of undiscovered secrets that Hunt could reveal in a deal to get less time. The CIA has a labyrinth of tunnels and private space in the building's basement. These were used to arrange off the book meetings. Hunt has been labeled as the Watergate mastermind. He has been credited with devising the plan and pulling together the crew that botched the burglary. Up until this point, Hunt has played his part and has kept his mouth shut, not divulging any information. The prolonged investigation has rendered Hunt and his family penniless. The expensive Potomac, Maryland lifestyle has caught up to the cash-strapped Hunt. He has gladly fallen on the President's sword, but he feels the need to be compensated for his troubles.

Director Carter walks into the CIA basement flanked by his security detail. As he gets further down the tunnel, Carter sees an image smoking in the distance. Carter asks his security detail to give him some space.

"Guys give me a moment," states Carter as he walks another 20 yards to an awaiting Howard Hunt.

"Howard," recites Carter.

"Director," says Hunt as the men shake hands.

"How are you holding up?" questions Carter.

"Things could be better," hints Hunt.

"What can I do for you?" requests Carter.

"I need money. No one returns my calls. They all are running scared. God damn it, Carter. I have kept my mouth shut. It is like I have been burned," expresses a flustered Hunt.

"I am sure it is just a misunderstanding. You have been very valuable," declares a reassuring Carter. "Director, you know I have always been loyal. I helped with the things in Dallas and Memphis, I helped with the thing at Chappaquiddick, how are they just going to throw me out to the wolves?" rambles Hunt.

"The thing in Chappaquiddick?" asks Carter.

"I guess they don't tell you everything. After Nixon won the election, he had a hit list. No one was going to get in the way of a second term. Baby Kennedy scared the bejesus out of Nixon. He swore 1960 wasn't going to happen again," says Hunt.

"Why was he doing that? He had won; he was the President," inquires Carter.

"He loves power. That power is intoxicating. He never wants to lose it," declares Hunt.

# MUNICH

The 20th Olympic games are in full swing. The games began on August 26th and are due to conclude on September 12th. The outlook for the games was to present an air of unity and peace. The previous games in 1968 were marred in controversy after John Carlos and Tommy Smith's silent protest in support of the Black Power movement. The International Olympic Committee vowed there would not be a repeat of those events. The first week of the games saw exciting contests with personal bests from: American Frank Shorter, who was the first American to win the coveted marathon race in 64 years and swimmer Mark Spitz who won seven gold medals. The German people have gone out of their way to make sure there was an air of inclusiveness. The German people wanted the 1972 games to be in complete contrast to Adolf Hitler's propaganda driven 1936 games in Berlin. Teed and Danya have enjoyed watching the games on TV thus far. It gave them a chance to kick back and forget the world's problems for a couple of weeks while getting more insight into each other. Danya was even more excited to see her god brother Liam's Israeli fencing team compete. Liam had been an above average fencer but developed into a great teacher and brought notoriety to the team.

Early in the morning of September 6th around 4:30 am, eight masked men stormed the rooms of some of the Israeli athletes taking 11 of them hostage. Within hours, the news came out that the Israeli athletes had been taken hostage and that the authorities were awaiting hostage demands. Teed and Danya awakened to the horrific news. They are watching TV when a broadcaster breaks in.

"We are following the breaking news that Israeli athletes have been taken hostage in their Olympic quarters. It is unknown at this time, if all the athletes are safe and exactly what the kidnappers want," reveals the news commentator.

Obviously, Danya can't get the information she wants. She picks up the phone and begins to dial.

"Who are you calling?" questions a concerned Teed.

Danya puts her finger on her lips asking Teed to be quiet.

"Madame Prime Minister please," requests Danya of the operator.

"You are calling a Prime Minister?" whispers Teed.

"Hello, Madame Prime Minister. Is there any news?" inquires a visibly shaken Danya.

She listens as the Prime Minister gives her instructions to stay put.

"Are we mobilizing?" asks Danya.

Danya listens intently to the instructions she is given.

"I understand and I will await your call," concedes an obedient Danya.

She hangs up the phone.

"What's wrong?" queries Teed.

"We aren't doing anything. The Germans don't have the knowledge to deal with this," snaps Danya.

The pair sits on the couch for the next 10 hours awaiting any news. At 9:55 pm, a news commentator interrupted the hours of continuously rehashed information. "Breaking news. We have received unconfirmed information that there has been an agreement with the terrorists," proclaims the commentator.

Danya and Teed continue to watch TV intently.

Minutes later there is movement on the TV screen, the terrorists directed the blindfolded hostages to awaiting helicopters. The helicopters flew the hostages and terrorists to Furstenfeldbruck Air Base a short 15 miles away. The agreement was that the terrorists would release the hostages at the air base once they had confirmation of their demands. The reality was the plan was doomed from the start. Upon arrival at the air base, two of the terrorists inspect the plane. The terrorists feel they are being set up. The two terrorists rush out of the plane to warn their companions of the apparent set up. Suddenly, the lights go out on the tarmac. Inexplicably bullets begin to fly in every direction. All of a sudden, an explosion fills the evening sky.

"Breaking news, we have news about the hostage situation. We have been told that the terrorists have all been killed and the hostages are saved," says the news anchor.

Danya immediately jumps into Teed's arms. "Thank God," conveys a relieved Danya.

The next morning Danya walks to the kitchen. The TV is on, she sees the Israeli flag flying at half-mast. Danya runs over to the TV; slowly she turns up the volume.

Olympic sportscaster Jim McKay states, "My worst fears have been realized. The 11 hostages have been killed. They are gone including the terrorists. They are all gone. ALL OF THEM!" reveals the exasperated Jim McKay.

"LIAM!" yells Danya.

# RACHE

The Olympic Massacre in Munich has been a blatant reminder of the world's continued Anti-Semitism. The Israelis and much of the world believed the 1972 Olympic games were to be an olive branch to the Jewish people. Many thought the games could serve as some sort of atonement for the horrendous events that occurred during the Holocaust. Israeli Prime Minister Golda Meir has been put in the unenviable position of being a politically correct head of state and the leader of a country that is clamoring for revenge. In the days following the massacre, Meir met with the top brass of her military and her government's intelligence agencies. She wanted to know her options and a possible course of action. During her tenure as Prime Minister, the Israeli people have looked at Meir as their collective mother. Meir has always been aware of this view of her, and she has embraced it. And much like a mama bear whose cubs have been attacked, the Prime Minister will not let the murders of the fallen go unavenged. Danya Franck has been summoned back to Israel to meet with the Prime Minister, she awaits her return from a meeting. Danya was not given details for the meeting, but she is hoping the Prime Minister wants her to be a part of the pending retribution. Danya is itching to be a part of any mission in response to the massacre. Prime Minister Meir walks in visibly worn out.

"Hello Dear," utters Meir as she gives Danya an embrace.

"Ma'am," says Danya as the Prime Minister walks behind her desk. She plops down in her office chair.

"This has been a great tragedy for our country. I am sorry I couldn't give you any details prior to now," admits an apologetic Meir.

"I completely understand Madame Prime Minister," responds Danya.

"I could not give you any details before because I didn't know what I was going to do. This massacre has brought back all the feelings from the Holocaust. They take our lives with impunity. They use us as the scapegoats for their deficiencies. Our lives seem to mean nothing to them. NO MORE!" proclaims a resolute Golda Meir.

Danya feels the Prime Minister's passion and wants to help bring her mission to fruition. "Ma'am, what do you want?" questions Danya.

"Rache. I want revenge. I want you to help me and Israel to get revenge," concedes Meir.

# WRATH

Israeli Prime Minister Meir has decided to put a plan in motion to exact revenge on everyone believed to be a part of the Olympic Massacre. No one will be spared, if you were a part of the planning, you die. If you provided the guns, you die. If you provided money, you die. There was to be no mercy of the perpetrators, no one would be allowed to hide behind ignorance of the details. Prime Minister Meir has enlisted super spy extraordinaire Mike Harari to map out the reprisal. Harari was known for running successful covert missions in foreign lands. Harari drew up plans for four teams of Mossad agents to survey the suspected perpetrators before killing them. Israel wanted to make sure they kept the moral high ground; only proven participants were to be eliminated.

Not officially a part of the missions, Harari asked Danya to eliminate the first name on the list, Wael Zwaiter. The semi-retired Danya Franck was chomping at the bit and wanted to strike a blow for Mother Israel and her friend Liam. The Mossad's intelligence tracked Zwaiter to Rome, Italy where he served officially as a translator for the Palestinian Liberation Organization (PLO). Days of surveillance revealed that Zwaiter loved to eat at different swanky Roman restaurants. He normally meets with a small contingent of Palestinians now living in Rome to hold court on the world view as he sees it.

"The Palestinian man and woman are the rightful heirs of the so-called holy land. Palestinians have recently been displaced from the very lands that they toiled over for centuries. Many would tell you that the Palestinian people and the Jewish people didn't get along. That is not entirely true. Many Jews left the area to prosper in foreign lands. They moved to Europe, to Africa and others lands far and wide. Were there fights? Were there disagreements? Absolutely. But the Palestinian people didn't evict the Jews. They left on their own accord abandoning the lands centuries ago. Twenty-five years ago, Zionists with the help of the colonizing United States of America, Great Britain and France thought they could just take our birthright without any consequences. They have discovered we are not a weak and not a forgiving people." remarks Zwaiter as the small group of onlookers applaud.

Danya is sitting in a small unassuming sedan watching Zwaiter at the outside Cafe.

"Ladies and gentlemen, I appreciate the meal and the conversation," says Zwaiter as he gets up from the table and begins to walk away. He walks about 100 yards to his favorite grocery store where he purchases a gallon of milk and a carton of eggs. Zwaiter leaves out of the store unaware that Danya is stalking him like large game. She is careful to remain vigilant of her surroundings, she wants to make sure she is not being tracked. Danya stays a safe distance from Zwaiter until he reaches his building. Danya picks up her pace in order to make sure she doesn't lose him while she walks into the building. There stands Zwaiter waiting for the elevator. The lobby is empty. It is just Danya and Zwaiter. She walks over to him.

"Excuse me, sir. Are you Wael Zwaiter?" probes Danya with a gentle tone.

"Why, yes. Yes, I am," admits a gentle Zwaiter.

Danya has the verification she needs. She pulls out a Beretta 77 and unloads 11 bullets into Zwaiter's body. Zwaiter drops the bag of groceries, breaking the bottle of milk and cracking several eggs out of the carton. Zwaiter's lifeless body lays in the pool of spilled milk and broken eggs. Danya stands over his body as he bleeds out thinking this murder will not make up for Liam's death. The Munich Massacre is still a collective slap at the Jewish people.

"For Liam," affirms Danya as she walks out of the lobby door.

# THE WARNING

Wafai Rashad knew that he was probably on some U.S. Government watchlist for his radical exploits, but he would have never thought it would be so extensive. The Hoover file had Wafai's information from his birth through Hoover's death. He knew if they had all his information, they would most certainly have the rest of Black September's information.

After learning about the investigation into his background, Wafai made a beeline for Rome. He knew that Black September chief strategist Wael Zwaiter was planning their next attack. Zwaiter was in the process of planning a hijacking of the Israeli airliner El Al. The preliminary plans called for hijacking one of the flights bound for the West. The flight would be rerouted to Damascus where Black September would begin negotiations for the plane and its passengers' release. They are hoping to have a number of British and American passengers. Westerners make good bargaining chips, so believe the radicals.

Danya Franck walks out of the lobby where she has just murdered Wael Zwaiter. Danya feels a major weight off her back with the execution of Zwaiter. That moment of overwhelming peace was interrupted when Danya spots Wafai Rashad about 100 yards away walking toward her. Danya starts to survey the area; she knows there's potential for a gun battle on the unsuspecting Rome street. As Wafai continues to walk toward Zwaiter's residence, he is overcome by an uneasy feeling. Wafai looks up and standing 50 yards away from him is Danya. Wafai recognizes her from the picture in the 8MEN file. Her face and searing eyes have been etched into his mind. A face he will never forget. Wafai knows Danya is an assassin and he knows he can't match her marksmanship. He pulls his gun and shoots anyway. The gun shots create instant hysteria. Wafai begins to run through the scattering crowd. Danya tracks the perfect shot of Wafai through the crowd like a trained dancer. Her glide through the crowd is as elegant as it is deadly as she is able to get off a clean shot hitting Wafai in the shoulder as he runs into an alley. Danya is in full pursuit as she hears the police coming, she puts her gun away and runs in the opposite direction.

"SHIT!" blurts out a frustrated Danya.

She knows she has missed a major opportunity and a target that may not come again.

# CAMP DAVID

President Nixon's staff wanted to get the President away from the fervor of the Watergate investigation. The constant questioning of the President and his staff have left little time for the other pressing business that the administration should be tending to. The overwhelming reelection victory of just two weeks ago has faded to the back of President Nixon's mind. The country has seemingly given the President a mandate to steer the country to his liking. The election was a sound thumping; it was never in danger of being lost. Over the last year, most polls had the President leading by no less than 20 percentage points over his Democratic rival during the lead up to Election Day. The President has executed many of the promises he campaigned on. He's brought some law and order to the United States while riding it to record popularity. With his election victory, Nixon started to think about his legacy. The Watergate inquiry has been kept at bay during the latter part of the campaign but now, with many of the perpetrators' trials coming up quite quickly, the focus will again switch back to the Watergate scandal. Nixon believed with his overwhelming popularity and his seemingly convincing thumping of McGovern; he hoped the country had put the scandal behind them as well. Director Wesley Carter did not usually accompany the President to Camp David, but the Director wanted to inform the

President of Howard Hunt's demands. "Director Carter, I want to thank you for holding the line throughout this whole Watergate thing. You have helped us tremendously," asserts a thankful President Nixon.

"Thank you, Mr. President. I met with Hunt. He is a true patriot," expresses Carter.

"That he is," agrees Nixon.

"He does have some concerns," conveys a concerned Carter.

"What concerns could he possibly have? We have gotten him the best defense possible money can buy. He shouldn't have to do too much time," hints a dismissive Nixon.

"I don't think the amount of time is bothering him. He wants to be well-compensated. As he has stated to me, he is not afraid of jail time. He wants to make sure his family is well taken care of," recites Carter.

"Of course, that is understandable. What number is talking about?" asks Nixon.

"He wants $500,000 to start. He will want more depending on his sentence," states Carter. "Outrageous. He is a patriot. He should be doing this for love of country. You know I worry. He needs to view this as a war. A war for the soul of America. That son of bitch has been around since the Truman administration. He has seen and knows a lot of our secrets. Watergate is just the tip of the iceberg. I would say just take them all out, but we don't want to run the risk of making them martyrs," says President Nixon.

"We need to tread lightly with him. He and the others must be given a message," replies a grim Carter.

# THE MESSAGE

The burglars involved in the Watergate break-in have become a bit anxious since the President's sizeable electoral victory. "The Plumbers," as the burglars have been affectionately referred to in the press, have begun to worry about going to prison without the compensation they were promised. The Plumbers thought they were instrumental in getting information on the President's Democratic rivals that allowed for the President's run-away victory. The Plumbers knew the possible risks of their clandestine missions, but knowing their families would be financially taken care of gave them solace in completing their tasks. Even though Director Carter had absolutely nothing to do with the Watergate burglary, he knew that Hunt held many of America's dirty little secrets. Carter knew that there was a spotlight on the so-called Plumbers, but he knew equally that a message had to be sent to show how deep they all were into this mess. Recently, Dorothy Hunt has been rumored to want to expose some of the U.S. Government's clandestine secrets. For Carter, exposing the third-rate burglary at The Watergate was not his concern. Carter knew Hunt, and The Plumbers knew about his and the 8MEN's involvement in the King and Kennedy assassinations, not to mention the failed attempt to assassinate Fidel Castro. Carter had a particular affection for Hunt, but he knew Dorothy had to be silenced. Unlike most spies, Hunt spoke to his wife about his covert missions. Dorothy did not appreciate that Howard was in her opinion, taking all the risk without realizing any of the rewards. The Hunts were by no means destitute, but they did not share in the wealth of Carter and his cronies. Dorothy has always felt that the government and the agency has always taken advantage of her husband. She felt he and by extension their family has sacrificed so much for this country without reaping any type of rewards. And Dorothy wants her reward. She is meeting with CBS reporter Karen Wilcox to discuss ghostwriting a book about an American spy's wife. Dorothy and Ms. Wilcox have discussed the possibility of the book for several months. Ms. Wilcox didn't take Dorothy seriously until she started giving certain details of E. Howard's escapades. Dorothy first described a fantastical story about the failed assassination attempt of Fidel Castro. Karen Wilcox thought Dorothy was full of shit, but the JFK story made her sit up and listen. Ms. Wilcox reached out to some contacts at the Pentagon to ask about some of Dorothy's details. The contact was floored by Dorothy's accuracy because most of the specifics weren't made public. Dorothy Hunt was spot on. She and Ms. Wilcox have been sitting on the plane for several minutes.

"Mrs. Hunt, I must say I thought you were fabricating your story," admits Karen Wilcox.

"I figured as much. But of course, you checked out my story. And you were amazed by my accuracy. There were things I told you that weren't in the news. So, us speaking about this is putting both of our lives at risk," suggests Dorothy.

"My publisher is looking at making an exclusive deal with you and possibly offering an option for a movie," recites Ms. Wilcox.

"Sounds good. Go ahead with your questions," states a confident Dorothy. "Let's start with the assassination of President Kennedy. Why did they do it?" inquires Wilcox.

"It all started with the failed Bay of Pigs operation. Howard said that the Kennedys fucked them. He didn't send them the proper military support for the operation. Many in the agency thought JFK and his brother Bobby were chicken shits. They were always worrying about the polls and how they would be seen. Kennedy was afraid of a war with Cuba. He knew that if he went to war with Cuba, he would be going to war with Russia. He wanted no parts of Russia. So, he left the American patriots to rot. The CIA and the soldiers didn't forget that," conveys a passionate Dorothy.

"So, the soldiers who were left in Cuba were a part of the assassination," probes Karen Wilcox.

"No, for the most part those soldiers were executed by the Cubans as traitors. Pretty much all of the soldiers that supported us were killed and branded as traitors. We gave our word that we would support them. Kennedy didn't want to get his hands dirty. Democracy is a dirty business, you must get some dirt on your hands from time to time," concedes an upset Dorothy.

In that instant, the plane started to shake. Ms. Wilcox looks out the plane window.

"What's going on?" demands a frantic Wilcox. "Somebody was told of your questions. Now they are cleaning up," declares Dorothy.

"Nobody knows I'm here," says Karen Wilcox.

"That is just naive. Once you verified my story. They probably had a person on you. Probably bugged your office at work and bugged your home. Waiting for the moment we were to meet. Lord, please bless my soul. I hope you are good with God," proclaims Dorothy as she is preparing to meet her maker.

The plane explodes, scattering debris and human remains.

# THE SWORD

The Plumbers are being sentenced for their crimes related to the break-in at the Democratic National Committee's office at The Watergate Hotel. The judge and the prosecutors have continually pleaded with Hunt and his co-defendants to tell who is pulling the strings. Hunt has been wavering since the death of his wife. He has been seriously thinking about telling his story, maybe writing a book. To this point, Hunt has not received any assistance from the President or any governmental organization. Dorothy's words rang in Hunt's ears, "you have given your life to this country. What have they given to you?" E. Howard Hunt arrived at the courthouse bright and early. He wanted to get his sentence, he knew he committed the crime, and he was going to do his time. But he knew that once he received his sentence, he no longer owed anyone his silence. As Hunt got out of the government car's back door, he notices Wesley Carter in a parked car across the street. Hunt gives Carter a look of disdain as the U.S. Marshalls usher him inside. Hunt's sentencing hearing was due to begin promptly at 9:30 am. The judge calls the court to order.

"We are here to pass judgment in the matter of the United States of America versus Everette Howard Hunt."

Hunt has changed from his prison jump suit to a tailored navy blue 3-piece suit.

"Do you want to use the bathroom before court?" asks one of the U.S. Marshalls.

"Sure, why not?" responds Hunt.

He walks down the short hallway, watched by the Marshall.

Hunt walks into the bathroom, and he sees Wesley Carter waiting. Hunt starts to charge Carter. Carter pulls out a .38 revolver and points it at Hunt.

"Howard, calm down. We need to talk," pleads Carter.

"You son of a bitch. Calm down? You killed Dorothy!" shouts an enraged Hunt.

The Marshall officers rush in. "Gentlemen, it is fine.

Everything is ok," responds panting Carter.

Hunt stops in his tracks. He knows the Marshall's deputies would smash him. "We are ok, correct?" asks Carter.

"Yes," replies a reluctant Hunt.

The Marshalls return to the hallway.

"Howard, you have to calm down," says Carter.

"You kill my wife, and you want me to be calm?" says Hunt.

"Howard," says Carter as he is interrupted.

"You have the gall to come here and ask me to do something. I'm not doing shit. The FBI wants to know what I know. God damn you and Nixon. I'm spilling the fucking beans. Let the chips fall where they may. All of you will be in cells right beside me," declares Hunt.

"Howard, that can't happen," states a solemn Carter.

"The hell it can't. I don't owe any of you a damn thing!" proclaims Hunt.

"Howard, Dorothy was going to write a book. She had a writer. It was being written. You know the rules," remarks Carter.

"I could have stopped her. She didn't need to die," expresses a sobbing Hunt.

"Howard, it is done. But you still need to be quiet and accept your sentence. Otherwise, your boy's safety can't be guaranteed," suggests Carter.

"Are you threatening my son?" demands Hunt as he walks toward Carter.

"Howard, this is beyond me. You talk, and the boy dies," claims a stern Carter.

Hunt shakes his head in disgust. "My fucking country," utters a frustrated Howard.

"It may not be worth anything to you right now, but I give you my word. If you accept the sentence nothing will come to your son," alleges Carter.

Carter extends his hand to shake it. Without a word, Hunt walks past Carter and walks out the bathroom door.

# THE DRAFT

The President has been in good spirits since the re-election festivities of last week's Inauguration. This day, January 27, 1973, will be an important date in American history. First, the Paris Peace Accords are being signed in an attempt to forge some semblance of peace in Vietnam. The peace accords were meant to establish a framework for the withdrawal of American troops from military engagement in the region. Secondly, as a byproduct of the ceasing of American military engagement in Vietnam, President Nixon's Defense Secretary Melvin Laird announced that the military would end the draft. President Nixon was keeping a campaign promise to end the overwhelmingly unpopular draft lottery. After the convictions and sentencing of several of the Watergate burglars without any mention of the President, the President was hoping that he could put the mention of scandals behind him. Unbeknownst to the Nixon administration, there was another scandal simmering out of the public eye. Vice President Spiro "Ted" Agnew was being investigated for bribery and possible tax evasion in Maryland. Agnew needed some advice on how to navigate this possible upheaval. A year ago, Agnew would have gone to Hoover for counsel but because of Hoover's death he is going to approach Director Carter. Wesley Carter is sitting in his office reading the paper when there is a knock on the door.

"Who is it?" asks Director Carter.

"Ted," responds the Vice President.

"Come in," utters Carter.

The Vice President enters Director Carter's office. Carter jumps to his feet.

"I hope I am not disturbing you," asks the soft-spoken Agnew.

"Of course not, what can I help you with?" asks Carter.

"I am really embarrassed by this...there may be a situation I have to deal with in the coming months," admits Agnew.

"Ok, how can I help?" questions Carter.

A paranoid Agnew paces back and forth.

"Could your office be bugged?" inquires Agnew. "Bugged, no sir," asserts a baffled Carter.

"There are people listening all the time, you know. Little listening devices," rambles a paranoid Agnew as he checks behind a lamp.

Carter is looking at Agnew with a strange expression.

"Sir, believe me this is office is not bugged. What can I help you with?" demands Carter as he begins to get annoyed.

"I am sorry to bring this to you, but I don't know where else to go," stammers Agnew.

"Sir, please," remarks Carter as he motions for Agnew to sit down.

"Ok. I am being accused of bribery during my time as Governor in Maryland." alleges Agnew.

"Do they have anything?" asks Carter.

"Not sure...aren't you going to ask?" utters Agnew.

"Ask what?" replies Carter.

"Ask if I did it," responds a curious Agnew.

"Sir, you wouldn't be here otherwise," says Carter matter of factly.

"What do I do?" questions Agnew as he drops his head in his hands.

"You need to fly under the radar. You are not a normal citizen. You are better off letting them come after you. Don't tip your hand. The administration doesn't need another scandal," asserts Carter.

"This Watergate thing seems like it is going away. The President won re-election nobody seems to care any longer," declares Agnew.

"Sir, I hope you are right. But these things have a way of turning on a dime," suggests Carter.

# YOM KIPPUR

The Middle East has been filled with tension since the creation of the state of Israel in 1947. There have been several large skirmishes over the past two decades. The most recent fracas, dubbed The Six-Day War of 1967, netted Israel, the all-important Sinai and the strategic stronghold of the Golan Heights from Syria. The Six-Day War increased Israel's territory four times. It is no secret that the Arabic states have suffered resounding losses to the Israeli military, nevertheless the current rhetoric continues toward war. Egyptian President Anwar Sadat has been hinting at peace with the Israelis for a couple of years now, with the caveat of Israel returning the lands captured in the war. Sadat promised to sacrifice a million soldiers if a peace treaty was not reached. Following President Nixon's directive, Director Carter sends Danya and Teed to Israel to get the temperature of the region. The U.S. has become Israel's primary ally, America is the primary military force that could back up the Israeli military in the event the Arab states overtake them. Danya and Teed have gone to the Israeli city of Eilat. Eilat sits at the Northern tip of the Dead Sea and at the southernmost end of the Negev Desert. Eilat was a perfect location for Danya and Teed to do recon on the Egyptian military's movement. The Egyptian city of Taba is a stone's throw away from Eilat. The Bible speaks of Eilat as the place the Israelites took their first steps onto the Promised Land as they escaped Pharaoh's army in Egypt. Teed is looking through binoculars onto the Gulf of Aqaba.

"You know this is the area the Bible says the Israelites took their first steps unto the Promised Land after their Exodus from Egypt," mentions Danya.

"Really. It looks like such a peaceful place," remarks a surprised Teed.

"Did you expect Jews and Arabs to be sitting on the border sword fighting?" wisely asks Danya.

Teed laughs, "No. There is just the perception of unending fighting here," he said.

"Make no mistake, violence can pop off at any time," responds Danya.

"I guess it is the unknown, huh?" suggests Teed.

"This is the thing that scares every Jew," concedes Danya.

"What scares you?" asks Teed.

"We just want to live in peace. The Arabs don't even want us to exist. On a normal day most of the Arabs can't agree on anything unless you are talking about the destruction of Israel," replies a saddened Danya.

"I've never understood why all the fighting," says Teed.

Danya looks at Teed with a condensing look.

"Think about it as the most complicated family feud. Of course, you know the story of Abraham in your Bible?" quizzes Danya.

"Sure, he was going to sacrifice his son Isaac, right?" claims Teed.

"Yeah, right. Well, you know Abraham had two sons Isaac and Ishmael. Long story short, Isaac became the father of the Jews and Ishmael became the father of the Muslims," says Danya.

"So, all this time you have been fighting your cousins," implies Teed.

Danya lets out a hearty laugh.

"I guess at some level but again, it is a little more complicated than that. It is a large family feud. But it was created by outsiders. In a way, I understand some of their animosity. After World War II, the British and your government started to divide up the holy land not understanding the history. In large part, the Jewish people left the holy land. The westerners knew we needed a safe homeland after the Holocaust. The Muslims sympathized with the Nazis, so their feelings were not taken into account. All the Arabs knew was we had taken their land, so we incurred their wrath at first. Now they understand, the Western governments played a part. This is just the beginning. The radicals want to destroy us all. Many of them are looking at this period as the next Holy Crusades," declares Danya.

"The Holy Crusades, like in the Bible?" asks a stunned Teed.

"Yes, those Crusades. History plays such a tremendous role. We fight them and they fight us. Nothing is ever solved. I fear we are doomed to repeat the horrors of our forefathers. War is on the horizon," asserts a prophetic Danya.

# BLACK GOLD

The aftermath of the Yom Kippur War was felt throughout the Arab world. Arabs from all walks of life were angered by the results of the War. Many of the Arabs weren't mad because the Jews and Palestinians were fighting. The war made the Arab world mad because many believed the scales were being tipped. Most Arabs saw the Palestinians losing The Six-Day War and even more so the Yom Kippur War as a result of the Westerners helping the Zionists. The radical extremists viewed this as the beginnings of their Jihad. The Jihad, or Holy War, as many extremists saw it, was the Jewish State of Israel with backing from the Americans, the Brits, and French governments against the people of Palestine. The other Arab countries of the region felt a kinship with their under-resourced Arab brothers. Along religious lines they all thought they had to fight or at least show their outrage.

On October 16, 1973, the Organization of Arab Petroleum Exporting Countries or OPEC enacted an oil embargo against the United States and Great Britain. The embargo halted oil exports and cut oil production. The embargo has sent the U.S. economy into a tailspin, the United States started to brace for a recession. America's dependence on foreign oil prompted many within and outside its government to pick up the phone and lobby members of the OPEC board to increase oil production. Lance Bowen has always had a chummy relationship with Prince Saud. The two men have had a lucrative relationship together making millions of dollars, but this crisis could test their relationship. Coincidentally, many of Bowen's Texas oil fields were producing less oil after an Indian Summer hurricane ravaged the Gulf Coast. The hurricane furthered the Bowen company's problem of getting fuel to their service stations and other gas outlets. Lance Bowen places a phone call to his old friend Prince Saud.

"Prince Saud how are you doing?" asks Bowen.

"Mr. Bowen, I am blessed. What do I owe for this pleasant surprise?" inquires Prince Saud.

"I wish it was purely a non-business call, but I was hoping you could help me. I need to find some petrol for my gas stations. My business is truly suffering. I was hoping there was some kind of way we could get some gas from your country," pleads Bowen.

"Mr. Bowen you are aware of the embargo?" asks Prince Saud.

"Yes, of course but I am pretty sure there is another way around it. We have to get some oil," requests Bowen.

"Well, umm," stammers Prince Saud.

"Anything you have will help," asserts Bowen.

"Well, there is a small country named Gabon. They are trying to become a player in the industry, but they aren't a member of OPEC yet," reveals Prince Saud.

"I never heard of that country before," remarks Bowen.

"The country is in the African sub-Saharan. Oil deposits were discovered there a little over a decade ago," affirms Prince Saud.

"I don't care where they are, I just need oil," proclaims Bowen.

"We are meeting some reps from the country in Zurich next week," mentions Prince Saud.

Bowen's mood changes from desperate to hopeful.

"Would it be ok if I came and possibly talk to them?" asks Bowen.

"I don't see why not. But please arrive very early because we may vote to have them join OPEC. Any deal they reach prior to the vote will be honored. After the vote, they too will no longer be able to sell to any American or British companies," claims Prince Saud.

# ZURICH

Zurich, Switzerland has become the unofficial capital of international business. The international hub has flourished because of the country's neutrality. Switzerland's neutrality has allowed political and business rivals the necessary space to work out difficult situations. The country's neutrality goes back to the time following the rule of the maniacal Napoleon Bonaparte. After Napoleon, European countries thought it would be valuable to have Switzerland serve as a mediating force for the region's volatile issues. Most recently, during World War II the Swiss were greatly criticized for their continued trade and alleged laundering of Nazi money. It was thought that Switzerland could again play host to some much-needed deal-making. The oil embargo is a strain for the U.S. and its allied countries, but it was also a liberation for the OPEC countries. Most of the OPEC countries were tired of America and the other western countries dictating sale terms, but the reality was that most of the oil output found its way to U.S. shores.

Lance Bowen raced through the Zurich Airport; he knew time was of the essence. Every minute that went by brought the Bowen Oil Company closer to going out of business. Bowen was hoping that Prince Saud's lead of getting oil from the country of Gabon would bare fruit. Bowen arrived at the Romaine Hotel a little after 10 am. He rushes to the 3rd floor where the meeting is taking place. As Bowen enters the room, the nation of Gabon agrees to join the OPEC countries. The Gabonian officials are signing documents and sipping champagne as their country's fortune will forever be changed. It is a festive atmosphere. But not for Lance Bowen. He knows that with the admittance to OPEC the Gabonians can no longer help him. So, where is he to turn?

"What the fuck!" exclaims a surprised Bowen as he watches his company's fate being sealed with the stroke of a pen.

Prince Saud walks over to Bowen to try to calm the situation.

"Mr. Bowen, we tried to wait for you. If you had made your deal before Gabon joined OPEC it could've been honored," hints an apologetic Prince Saud.

The frustration is evident on Bowen's face.

"You should have waited. All the money I have spent on you and all these fucking sheepherders in this room. You all owe me this fucking oil," expresses an exasperated Bowen.

The level of disrespect is written all over Prince Saud's face. His shock has rendered him speechless and motionless. A short distance away is the prince's cousin Wafai Rashad. The cousins share a head nod to let each other know something needed to be done about Bowen's disrespect. Bowen storms out of the meeting. As he leaves the meeting, he gives his coat and briefcase to his driver.

"Hold this, I gotta take a piss," says a rude Bowen.

Bowen is in the bathroom taking a piss and continuing to rant.

"Fucking niggers and Arabs have ruined me. Gave them too much money. Can't fucking believe it. The country should just take the fucking oil," declares an upset Bowen.

As Bowen turns around, he sees a Middle Eastern man looking back at him.

"What do you want?" questions Bowen.

"I wanted to know what entitlement looked like," rebuts Wafai.

"What?" asks a puzzled Bowen.

"Your company has been robbing the people of the Middle East for decades. You give a mere pittance to the Arab countries compared to your profit, but you still feel like we owe you. But at some point, you and those from your country will get tired of paying even the pittance and will try to take the oil from us like your grandfather did to the indigenous Americans in Oklahoma," alleges Wafai.

"You dare disrespect my family?" says Bowen.

"This is so far past disrespect," proclaims Wafai as he pulls out a revolver. Wafai points and shoots Bowen three times, one in the forehead and two to the chest. He falls to the floor as he lays in a pool of his blood. Wafai spits in the direction of Bowen as he walks out of the bathroom.

# LIMBO

The death of Lance Bowen was not as consequential to the 8MEN as the two prior deaths of Senator Hampton Capers and FBI Director J. Edgar Hoover. But Bowen's murder left the group with many more questions about why he was killed and who killed him. The 8MEN were unsure if Bowen's murder was connected to them or was it an old, unsettled score of his own making. The Bowen name in Western Texas was not a celebrated name but more of a necessary evil. The family patriarch Irving Bowen, Lance Bowen's grandfather, was a hardware store owner in the beginning of the century. Irving was a struggling hardware business owner when a customer he was delivering lumber to ask if wanted to purchase his property. The property owner was tired of dealing with the black liquid flowing on his property. Bowen bought the land for pennies on the dollar. In the years to come, Irving Bowen sold his hardware business and began an oil drilling business. Because he got in on the ground floor, he saw his profits grow exponentially. The elder Bowen tried to purchase tracts of land from other landowners without much success. Others in western Texas wanted the same success that Bowen had achieved so the prices of land skyrocketed. Bowen would not be deterred, so he began a campaign of terror by murdering and destroying the property owners. Not to be out done, Marshall Bowen, Lance's father learned at the feet of his father. Marshall expanded the Bowen brand into southeastern Oklahoma. The land was ripe with oil and was owned by Native Americans. It has been long rumored for years that Marshall Bowen with the help of Irving instigated a massacre of several tribes in southeastern Oklahoma. After the massacre, the Bowen family became the owners of several large tracts of land previously owned by the Osage Indian Tribes. Needless to say, the Bowen family has created its own hatred, but was it Karma or something with the 8MEN that got Lance Bowen killed?

The funeral of Lance Bowen is a very low-key service with a low turnout at Bowen's family church and the cemetery established by Bowen's grandfather. Director Wesley Carter, Cecil Thomas and Murray Smith pay their respects to the Bowen family. The service is being held at the Mount of Olives Baptist Church in Austin, Texas. The Bowen family has been the sole benefactor of the beautiful church filled with stained glass windows and beautiful marble steps and altar. The small quaint service was attended by some of the Bowen family and some church parishioners. A large part of the Bowen family was not in attendance for good reason. Lance Bowen orchestrated a hostile takeover of the family company several years back leaving several members of his family penniless. After his death, the local newspaper reported that one of his disgruntled relatives thought the oil baron was the victim of Karma on the European continent.

Director Carter, Cecil Thomas and Murray Smith paid their respects and are getting in their limousine riding back to the airport.

"Did you ever find out who killed Bowen?" asks Murray Smith of Director Carter.

"No. Bowen had a lot of enemies. If they weren't ones he made, they were enemies his daddy or his granddaddy made. The Bowens were not well-loved people, no disrespect," expresses Director Carter.

"Bowen was a dick, and I heard his daddy was a dick too, but we need to know what happened," proclaims Cecil Thomas.

"We had some intel that revealed some issues with some Africans over some oil fields in Sub-Saharan Africa. The oil shortage displayed some real issues with Bowen's company. Many of the Bowen stations ran into trouble supplying gas. It would have gotten better over time, but the shortage was hurting Bowen's reputation. And Bowen didn't want that to be an issue," says Director Carter.

"I will put some reporters on the story," claims Murray Smith.

"No matter what happened we need to know," replies Thomas.

"I will also see if Teed and Danya can find any leads," says Carter.

# THE LUMIERE

In 1973, the U.S. Department of State commissioned a report on the world's population. The report concentrated on the Earth's population as it relates to the use of its natural resources. The use of the world's natural resources has steadily increased since the end of World War II. The report concludes that there is a correlation between there being no large global military action in the last 30 years and the rising depletion of natural resources. The classified report suggests that there will need to be an event to decrease the world's rising population. It has been proposed that some kind of pathogen be introduced to a vulnerable subset of the populace in order to slow mankind's pending tipping point.

The recent upheaval in the world has spawned several groups of elites to look into limiting the world's population. The elites have looked at the recent famines in Africa, the oil shortage, civil and social unrest in the United States as signs of a need to limit the steady rising of human growth throughout the world. Director Carter was invited to a meeting of the Lumiere.

The Lumiere is a group of elites from all walks of life. Until recently, the group was made up of aristocrats, members of generational syndicates and the upper echelon of the world's clergy. The purpose of the group was to make and set rules across Europe, Asia and Northern Africa to limit any mass fluctuations in the markets and to identify any sudden uprisings. Even during World War II, the group prepared for both an Allied Victory as well as an Axis victory. The rumored inclusion of Nazis at the highest levels of the group has made many feel uncomfortable about the group's motives.

The Lumiere is meeting at Chalef du Mont d'Arbois in France. Director Carter has attended several of the day's meetings and seminars. Director Carter is in awe of all the influence and power at the meetings. Carter was familiar with all the concentrated power in America and much of the intelligence and military power in Europe and Asia. But this group represented the power and influences going back to Europe's dark ages. The group's overall objective was to stay in power and to extend their influence onto their children and proxies.

The Lumiere did not care what the form of government was capitalism, fascism, socialism, communism or the aristocracy, their objective was to rule. Capitalism posed a particular problem for the group's world dominance. The emergence of capitalism allowed for a more random chance for those outside of the Lumiere to succeed. The Lumiere wanted more order and an overall plan for the world's wealth and influence. Director Carter walks outside after one the sessions to get a smoke. Carter is approached by a gentleman in his late 60's.

"How are you enjoying our conference?" asks Fritz Khan.

"It has been very interesting to say the least," responds Carter.

"I am glad you are interested," replies Kahn.

Carter has no idea who Kahn is, he looks away and takes another smoke.

"The work your group is doing is also quite interesting," remarks Kahn.

Carter gives Kahn a scowling look.

"Look, I am an admirer. Your group is taking action. You decided on a course of action, then executed it," suggests Kahn.

"I think you have me confused with someone else." mentions a coy Carter.

"Maybe, but your supposed group is strategically well-placed. To have effectively infiltrated the most powerful agencies within your government and to incorporate the most powerful and lucrative business minds within your country and co-opted the media…simply brilliant," said Kahn.

"If I come across this supposed group, I will inform them of your admiration," says Carter as he walks away.

"We will see each other again soon," Kahn whispers to himself.

# THE POWER

The 1970s have been a turbulent period for the U.S. as a whole, but even more for the newly lamented African Americans, formerly known as Negroes. The aftermath of the death of Martin Luther King Jr. was more far reaching to the psyche of the African American people than first thought. The once docile group of Americans who followed the nonviolent approach of Martin Luther King has abandoned his teachings for the "By Any Means Necessary" approach advocated by one-time leader of the Nation of Islam, Malcolm X.

The frustration of the African American people after the riots of 1968 led many activists to form organizations with the hopes of uplifting the race. Some of the organizations wanted to cultivate political power and others just simply wanted to stick their collective fingers in the white man's eye. The Eagle's Eye was an offshoot group of revolutionaries that left the Black Panther Party because of the Panthers' stance on white people assisting the cause. The Eagle's Eye stayed away from the controversial stance against the police and symbols of white oppression that the Black Panther Party constantly challenged. The Eagle's Eye concentrated on shedding light on the hypocritical American Government and the racist approach to law enforcement in the U.S. Anthony Montgomery has risen to a leadership role within the Eagle's Eye because of his knowledge of the inner workings of the federal government. Montgomery did not share the Black Panthers' "in your face" approach, he knew that sooner or later the group would be infiltrated corrupting their message. The Eagle's Eye has been doing low level burglaries of law enforcement agencies looking for evidence of public corruption. After the burglaries, the Eagle's Eye has been feeding its stolen information to independent newspapers all over the U.S. Montgomery's time working undercover for the FBI taught him that the major media outlets were partners with corrupt government officials.

"How is everyone doing this evening?" asks Montgomery of the 200-plus people in attendance.

The crowd murmurs, "Ok."

Montgomery continued, "The community needs to come together. This fall we need to show our political power. You need to vote for people that act in your interest. If the dog catcher is not working for you, then you need a dog catcher that acts for you. This thought should be followed for all elected officials that supposedly represent you. Get involved, you must get involved!" Montgomery continues to chant, "get involved," when he sees Teed in the back of the crowd. Teed waits around until the rally is over. Montgomery greets Teed.

"Hey, what are you doing here?" asks Montgomery as he embraces Teed.

"I thought I would look in on you," says Teed.

"Glad you came by," mentions Montgomery.

"So, you are a voting rights activist?" queries Teed.

"I guess I'm trying to give back. People are asleep, they need to wake up. This government, this country. We can't bitch about the politicians if we aren't asking them what they stand for," preaches Montgomery.

"I am happy for you. Keep up the good work," declares Teed as he shakes Montgomery's hand.

Teed turns to leave.

"Does me being alive present a problem for me and you?" questions Montgomery.

"No, we both have paid for that debt. But be careful," says a smiling Teed as he leaves.

# THE PIGS

The citizens of the United States have been glued to their televisions over the past several months watching the real-life soap opera of the Senate Investigation into the break-in at The Watergate Hotel. The Senate hearings have gone from a widely considered witch-hunt to all the key witnesses admitting their roles, and they are beginning to implicate the President in the Watergate break-in cover-up. The recent revelation that President Nixon kept tapes of his conversations in the oval office has sparked interest from Congress followed by a subpoena to listen to the tapes.

The overwhelming support Nixon felt after his landslide victory in the election of 1972 has all but vanished. The once hardened Nixon supporters from just 18 months ago are now talking impeachment. Impromptu protests and rallies denouncing the President are popping up all over the country, but the District of Columbia is the epicenter of the impeachment effort. Anthony Montgomery has brought members of his Eagle's Eye organization to Washington, D.C. to protest.

On this beautiful 15th day of July, the Eagle's Eye has organized a rally at the Ellipse near the White House. The hopes of this festive atmosphere were to capture the attention of the local constituency. The is event headlined by local musical artists, including Chuck Brown and the

Soul Searchers, Roberta Flack, and Donny Hathaway. The Eagle's Eye has recently been leading local voting drives. The group has been trying to get the community to vote. Since the passage of the Voting Rights Act, Black people have been gaining a presence in politics. Anthony Montgomery has taken to the microphone to help encourage the crowd.

"Brothers and sisters, we are here today to protest the authoritative state of the United States. Across the street sits a man that has given orders to the pigs to harass those who don't support the military industrial complex. We must stay strong and demand that Congress rid us of this President but let us take this time to also denounce the pigs who act out brutal attacks on the population in this President's name," states Montgomery with many police officers from Washington, D.C. and the surrounding jurisdictions looking on.

Later the same evening, Anthony Montgomery and Sandy Stewart are leaving a reception for activists. The reception was held to thank the activists for participating in today's rally. The local rally leaders wanted the activists to go home and get people in their towns to keep up the pressure on the Congress to get rid of the President. The reception was being held at the VFW building in College Park, Maryland, a short 15-minute ride from today's rally site.

Montgomery and Sandy are riding along Baltimore Avenue in the Hyattsville section of Prince George's County, Maryland. Montgomery pulls up to a red traffic light. Sitting at the traffic light are Prince George's County police officers, Captain Stephen King, and Lieutenant Michael Slager. Both men are 10-year veterans of the Prince George's County Police department. The officers have received many commendations for their great work including King's commendation for saving the life of a bank employee during a failed bank robbery in Greenbelt, Maryland. The officers have also had their share of complaints against them. Lt. Slager has been accused of excessive force by the Black Student Union at the

University of Maryland after Slager beat a young Black student after students of different races celebrated a University of Maryland basketball win. Only the Black student was injured. Slager and King are in the middle of a conversation at the light when Slager notices Montgomery.

"Look over there. Let the coons into our schools and universities and then they want our women," alleges Slager.

Captain King takes another look over at Montgomery.

"Wait a minute, that son of a bitch was one of the speakers at that impeachment rally today. He was the one that said we were pigs," declares King.

The light turns green Montgomery doesn't realize he has been profiled. The police pull off slightly slower than Montgomery's car.

"Let's teach that nigger a lesson," suggests Slager.

"Call it in," replies King.

Prince George's County, Maryland is a county in racial flux. The county went from a mostly rural existence to an up-and-coming metropolitan area. The county's proximity to Washington, D.C. and its exploding Black federal government workforce have put pressure on the county's changing racial make-up. Many of the white residents felt displaced by the perceived invading Blacks.

Montgomery continues to drive along Baltimore Avenue when he notices the blue and red lights of a police car.

"Shit!" exclaims Montgomery.

"Are you speeding?" quizzes Sandy

"No, but that doesn't really matter," says Montgomery as he starts to realize the severity of the situation.

Montgomery pulls the car over; he takes his license out and places his hands on the steering wheel. Captain King and Lieutenant Slager approach Montgomery's car with their revolvers drawn.

"Put your hands on the dashboard. Do it slowly," pleads Montgomery to Sandy.

Reluctantly, Sandy puts her shaking hands on the dashboard.

"We haven't done anything wrong," whispers Sandy as the officers approach the car.

"License," demands Captain King.

Montgomery hands Captain King his license while trying not to make eye contact with the officer.

"Excuse me officer, what did I do wrong?" questions Montgomery.

"You appeared to be weaving. So, we wanted to make sure you weren't under the influence of any drugs or alcohol," alleges Captain King.

Montgomery shakes his head in disbelief of Captain King's assertion. Lieutenant Slager knocks on the passenger window.

"Roll down the window," orders Lieutenant Slager.

Sandy slowly rolls down the window.

"Are there any drugs in the vehicle?" probes Slager.

"Absolutely not," responds Sandy.

"Mr. Alfred Green of 3441 Rockaway Avenue in Annapolis, Maryland. What are you doing in Hyattsville? You are a long way from home," implies Slager.

"Mr. Officer, we haven't had any drugs or alcohol or anything," asserts Montgomery.

"Ok, I will let you prove it," remarks King.

King pulls Montgomery's door open, "I want you to walk a straight line behind your car."

Captain King walks Montgomery behind the car.

"Are you being held against your will," asks Slager of Sandy.

"No," responds Sandy.

Sandy is fed up with the police officers; she pushes the door open and rushes behind the car.

"What is the reason for this? We haven't done anything wrong," states a frustrated Sandy.

"Ma'am, you are gonna have to go back to the car," says Captain King.

"No," responds Sandy.

Lieutenant Slager grabs Sandy by her hair.

"He told you to go back to the car," proclaims Lieutenant Slager as he slings Sandy to the ground.

Up to this point, Montgomery has been even tempered but now his emotions have gotten the best of him.

"What the fuck is your problem?" challenges Montgomery as he pushes Slager.

Slager falls to the ground.

"You fucking NIGGER, you pushed me," says Slager as he fires his gun three times.

All three shots hit Montgomery in the chest. Montgomery's body is thrown several feet to a resounding thud as he hits the ground. Sandy rushes to Montgomery's side, after a few screams asking him to get up Sandy realizes he is dead. Sandy screams out as she runs toward Slager. Captain King tries to stop Sandy but Lieutenant Slager fires two shots at Sandy, both hitting her in the chest, killing her instantly.

"What the hell did you do, Slager? You said you just wanted to teach them a lesson but this? FUCK!" exclaimed King as he looks at the bleeding bodies of Montgomery and Sandy.

"We have to figure something out. We are both in this thing together. If I go down, we go down." proclaims Slager.

# THE PRESSURE

A little over 18 months ago, the Nixon White House referred to the break-in at The Watergate Hotel and Office complex as a third-rate burglary. The investigation into the break-in has already yielded the convictions of G. Gordon Liddy and James McCord, former Nixon aides. With the convictions of Liddy and McCord, the White House is hoping these sacrificial lambs will take some of the political pressure off the President. Nixon is starting to feel the pressure of the constant inquiry into his role in the crime. There is a steady drumbeat by the Congress toward the impeachment of Richard Nixon.

President Nixon has convened a meeting of some trusted advisers in the basement of the White House to strategize about his situation. The President has invited Wesley Carter and Alexander Haig to help him come up with a solution. Haig has become the Nixon Chief of staff after the resignation of H.R. Haldeman. Haig has come up as a career military man, service to the President is but an extension of the same military oath as he sees it. The President has found himself in a very tough position. It has been discovered that the President installed a recording system in the Oval Office without informing any of his senior and mid-level staff. What he thought would be used to bolster political legacy may now cement his political downfall.

"What do I do? Do we give them the tapes?" asks Nixon.

"Mr. President, what will be your exposure?" quires Haig.

"Who the hell knows? I know I didn't tell anyone to break into the DNC, but there could be some other unsavory conversations on there," admits Nixon.

"Mr. President, did you make your staff feel like you wanted information about the Democrats at all costs?" questions a stern Carter.

Wesley Carter understands that powerful men don't necessarily have to tell their underlings to specifically commit a crime. All the President had to do was imply that he wanted something nefarious done.

"Mr. President, of course you didn't demand any of your staff to commit any crimes," communicates a naïve Haig.

Carter and President Nixon catch eyes. The two of them realize the severity of the on-coming situation.

"Al, can you give me and Director Carter a minute?" asks a soft-spoken President Nixon.

Al Haig excuses himself and leaves the basement.

"So, Carter, what do I do?" inquires Nixon as he walks to a nearby liquor cabinet and begins to take shots of liquor from an unlabeled bottle.

Mr. President, I really don't know. You recorded conversations in the Oval for over two years, without anyone knowing," responds Carter.

The President takes another large gulp of liquor before saying, "I never thought anything like this could have happened."

Carter asks, "But what was the upside? The conversations you had there. No President should record his most intimate meetings. Sir..." Carter is interrupted. "JUST HELP ME GOD DAMMIT!" bursts out the President. Carter is somewhat startled.

"I'm sorry, I don't know what else to do," concedes a conciliatory President Nixon.

"I don't know wh..." Carter is interrupted.

"Maybe we can use your people. They did a masterful job on the Kennedy boys and King," utters a terrified Nixon.

"What?" inquires an insulted Carter.

"I was thinking they could knock off those two reporters from The Post and one of The Plumbers to send some kind of a message for everyone to keep quiet," states a rambling Nixon.

"No...Mr. President, you can't murder your way out of this. Too many people know the secrets. Don't make this any worse. Negotiate with the Congress. Talk to Ford. Sir, you are going to have to give up the Presidency. Don't allow them to drag you out of here," declares a sobering Carter. The President realizes that he must end this nightmare.

# IMPEACH

The 8MEN have been preoccupied with the possibility of President Nixon being impeached, the fallout from Daniel Bowen's death, and the inevitable end of the Vietnam War. The country is caught up in the Watergate drama. The President's refusal to release the tapes of his conversations has made Washington, D.C. and by default the country, desperate to find out what is on the Nixon tapes. Several Republican Senators and elder statesmen have set a meeting with the President to help resolve the current situation. The possible impeachment of Richard Milhous Nixon was the primary story on all three Washington, D.C. television stations but WRC-TV4, the NBC affiliate, was carrying a story about a police shooting in Hyattsville, Md.

The Washington Sun ran a story in the morning edition about a police shooting of a Black man and a white woman who were resisting arrest. Outspoken WRC Black anchor Jim Vance is listening to the field reporter's report that was given by the police.

"The police are reporting that officer Slager feared for his life when both the man and woman charged him," says the Channel 4 reporter Chip Grigsby.

"Have the police found any weapons that the couple may have had?" questions Vance.

"Jim, the police did not mention a weapon," states Grigsby.

"No weapon. You are telling me they felt scared when there was no gun? Something doesn't sound right. Chip, please stay on this story," as a noticeably incensed Vance continues the broadcast.

"Will do, Jim." answers Chip.

Teed begins to turn the channel.

"Nothing but Nixon is on TV."

Danya is groaning in her sleep.

"Are you, okay?" asks Teed.

Danya awakes and rises out of the bed holding her stomach. She continues to groan.

"What was in those Margaritas you bought last night?" asks a pain-riddled Danya.

"The same liquor we normally get," responds Teed.

Danya feels an enormous amount of pressure in her stomach. She fears she is about to have a massive bowel movement. She believes the liquor she drank last night is the cause. The pain continues to build in Danya's stomach area. She rushes to the bathroom to sit on the toilet. Danya looks into the toilet bowl and sees blood and something resembling tissue and blood clots. She faints, falling off the toilet onto the floor.

"RICHARD!" screams a horrified Danya as she lays on the floor.

Teed runs into the bathroom.

"Danya, what is wrong?" asks Teed.

"I didn't know," says Danya as she rolls on the floor in pain.

# HERSTORY

anya Franck has been a consequential and deliberate steward of world events over the last quarter of a century. Danya has helped to liberate humanity from the grips of Adolf Hitler's Nazi regime, but she has also been responsible for extinguishing two of America's greatest beacons of change. Danya's life and existence has been quite complicated. She is probably the world's greatest spy, if not, she is certainly the greatest female operative to have ever lived. Danya's story is not simply about her being a great spy, but the events that forced this life upon her.

Danya's parents' position as doctors working with the Nazis allowed them to shelter her away from much of the day-to-day horrors the Nazis were inflicting on the average Jew. But that all changed after the murder of her parents and the attempted gang rape of Danya. After her parents were murdered, the guards thought they would molest the 16-year-old virgin before they executed her. They began to ravage the diminutive Danya when she summoned the fighting spirit of Joan of Arc. She savagely killed all her intended rapists with a dull butter knife. The Nazi rapists failed at killing Danya, but something in her died in those moments.

An unconscious Danya lays in an ambulance speeding toward Howard University Hospital. She has been bleeding for a little over 15 minutes. Teed anxiously sits in the ambulance watching the emergency medical techs try to stabilize her. One of the emergency workers is working nervously to stop the bleeding. "What's wrong?" questions Teed as he can see the workers' terror-stricken expression.

"I'm doing everything I can to save the baby," replies the tech worker as their words continue to echo in Teed's ears.


Later in the evening, a confused Danya awakens in a hospital bed.

"Where the hell am I?" demands a startled Danya.

Teed rushes to calm her down.

"You are in the hospital," says Teed.

"For what?" asks Danya.

Teed looks into the crackled ceiling searching for the right words to say.

"You were bleeding heavily," discloses Teed.

"Bleeding… and I had to come to the hospital?" nervously asks Danya.

Teed is searching for the strength to tell Danya the whole truth. But he doesn't know the whole truth. When did she get pregnant? Was it boy or a girl? Could he have done anything different? But none that matters right now. He needed to put all that to the side to make sure Danya was going to be ok.

"You had a miscarriage. You lost the baby," admits Teed as tears begin to roll down his face.

"No…no…no!" exclaims Danya as Teed holds her.

# DEAD INNOCENCE

It has been a little over a week since Anthony Montgomery and Sandy Stewart were killed suspiciously by police officers from the Prince George's County Police Department. Montgomery had been masquerading around as Alfred Green for the last three years, but because of the autopsy's proof on identification his identity was proven to be Anthony Montgomery. Montgomery was said to have been killed in a fire in Southeast Washington, D.C. in 1968. Unless Montgomery was Lazarus this time, he would stay dead.

The date of August 8, 1974 will go down in American history as one of the most important dates in the country's Presidency. Today, President Richard Milhous Nixon would be the first American President to resign from the post. In a short three hours, Nixon would be leaving the White House for presumably his home in California. The double funeral for Anthony Montgomery and Sandy Stewart was taking place while the United States moved through a constitutional crisis. The Mount Calvary Baptist Church in Northeast Washington hosted the sparsely attended funeral of Montgomery. Some of Montgomery's revolutionary buddies attended the funeral but there was no large contingent of family and/or friends to talk about. Teed and Danya walk into the funeral already in progress. The fiery pastor of Mount Calvary, Maurice Carrington, is trying to deliver an uplifting homegoing service.

"Anthony and Sandy were shot down allegedly by two officers while minding their own business. Anthony had been an FBI agent tasked with protecting Martin Luther King Jr. He tried to protect our Black messiah, but like Jesus Christ himself, Martin Luther King's destiny was pre-determined. Anthony and Sandra will be granted eternal peace. Mrs. Cheryl Montgomery, your son has done God's work. His soul will be rewarded by our lord. Keleeha your parents will be in heaven waiting to meet you," recites Pastor Carrington.

Anthony Montgomery has a child, instantly Teed starts to look at every move the child makes. Keleeha is a spirited four-year-old, she is running around the church unattended. Keleeha has been jockeyed to different people since her parents' death. She has been with Anthony's mother since her arrival. Mrs. Cheryl Montgomery is in her early 70s, she cares for Anthony's ailing stepfather and is raising Anthony's teenage niece and two nephews. Keleeha runs toward the back of the church. She and Danya catch eyes. Danya waves to the carefree child. Keleeha wants to play hide and seek with Danya without regard to the ceremony that is going on. They go back and forth putting their hands over their eyes continuing the game. The stress of Danya's own situation has been lifted by the simple smile of Keleeha.

After the funeral, Teed walks over to Mrs. Montgomery to offer her his condolences. Mrs. Montgomery is surrounded by her son's revolutionary cohorts sharing stories about his heroism and his leadership. As Teed walks up to Mrs. Montgomery everyone else leaves.

"Mrs. Montgomery, I want to offer my sincere condolences," conveys Teed.

"Thank you, Mr. Teed," responds Mrs. Montgomery.

Teed is surprised Mrs. Montgomery knows who he is.

"We have never met before, correct?" asks Teed.

"No, but my son spoke about you. He said if ever something happens to him to get in touch with you," comments Mrs. Montgomery.

"But ma'am," says Teed before he is interrupted.

"By the time I was getting ready to call you, I received a message that you had taken care of all the funeral arrangements. Thank you," reveals Mrs. Montgomery as she gives Teed a big hug.

"It was the least I could do," replies Teed.

"You did a lot, he told me you saved his life. You were like his guardian angel," expresses a thankful Mrs. Montgomery.

Teed starts to feel guilty. He wonders if he put Montgomery on the path to his death. In a moment of solace, Teed notices Danya and Keleeha playing patty cake together and starts to smile.

"I didn't know he had a daughter," utters Teed.

"Don't feel bad. I had not met her before today," reveals Mrs. Montgomery.

"So will she be going to North Carolina with you?" inquires Teed.

"I'm not sure. I don't think I can care for a toddler. But I can't just leave her," concedes Mrs. Montgomery.

Teed continues to watch Danya and Keleeha playing and laughing together.

# BURIAL

The burial of Anthony Montgomery has just concluded. Pastor Carrington is walking Mrs. Montgomery back to her car leaving Teed staring at Anthony Montgomery's head stone.

"You know I always knew bringing you into that King mess was wrong. I thought in some strange way by giving you money that would right the wrong. You were innocent to all this, but you paid the ultimate price. I gotta do something to make this right," declares Teed as he watches Danya and Keleeha continue their day-long game of hide and seek. The laughs and smiles from Danya and Keleeha bring a smile to Teed's face.

"If you talk to graves too long, they begin to talk back," remarks Director Wesley Carter.

The appearance of Director Carter has brought a sobering outlook for Teed.

"Director Carter," says Teed.

"Well, for a couple more hours," utters Director Carter as he checks his watch.

"You are resigning?" asks Teed.

"Yeah, it is time for a new path," replies Carter.

"So, this is the end of the 8MEN?" questions Teed.

"Not really, just a change of how we do things," remarks Carter.

"Are you here to kill me for not following your order to kill Montgomery?" asks Teed.

"No, of course not. Do you honestly believe I didn't know he was still alive?" divulges Carter as he chuckles.

"How long have you known?" asks Teed.

"About a year after he was supposed to be dead. An informant we planted in the Panthers told us," admits Carter.

Teed thinks about when he told Montgomery to hide and not to be seen again.

"I understand why you didn't do it. This covert business can be bullshit at times. He was a good man trying to do a good thing. The two of you were kindred spirits that way. All is forgiven...So what now?" requests Carter.

I don't know?" mentions Teed as Danya and Keleeha smile back at him.

"Take some time off," says Carter.

"I need you to pull some strings for me," suggests Teed.

"Depends on the strings," responds Carter.

"I need a new identity," says Teed.

"If you're getting out, why do you need a new identity?" asks Carter as he sees Teed smiling at Danya and Keleeha.

"I understand, I will get working on it. I owe you both that much," comments Carter as he gives Teed an affectionate tap on the back.

# DOWN & OUT

It has been a short four weeks since President Richard Nixon resigned. The country is still trying to recover after The Watergate scandal. The entire government is trying to collectively right the ship away from the perceived mess President Nixon and his administration left behind. Former CIA Director Wesley Carter has let a little bit of time pass before convening a meeting of the remaining 8MEN. The normally confident Carter didn't know what direction the 8MEN would now go in. Carter knew that President Ford would be pushed by public opinion toward ending the Vietnam War, ending the group's primary cash cow. President Nixon, the 8MEN thought, would be the perfect champion of their cause and their pursuit of wealth but he was the actual reason for their demise. Carter started to think that he and the 8MEN have wrongly put their fortunes in the hands of wayward politicians. Although from differing political persuasions, both President Kennedy and President Nixon have ruined the group's geopolitical goals. Carter realized that if the 8MEN were going to come there would have to be a plan to make things happen their own. They could no longer depend on politicians promises, they simply needed to make it happen.

Carter arrives at the 8MEN's meeting place in Northwest Washington, D.C. There is not the normal discussion, the room resembled a funeral service.

"Why so glum, gentlemen?" asks Carter.

"Haven't you been reading the paper?" challenges Cecil Thomas as he flings the day's edition of the Washington Sun in Carter's direction.

"You look quite tan, have you been on vacation?" asks Valerius Torrantio.

Carter retorts, "Let me answer all of your questions. No, I haven't been reading the news and no I haven't been on vacation. I really need to go though. And let me answer the collective question in your minds now. You are thinking 'what we are going to do now?' I share your angst toward the future. There are some realities we need to face. The Vietnam War is going to end next year. President Ford has all but guaranteed it. Hey, it was going to happen at some point. I have left government; I won't have immediate resources of the government, but I still have friends," affirms Carter.

"Is there something we can do to keep the war going?" asks Cecil Thomas.

"Cecil my friend, the Vietnam War was a great gravy train for us all, but it must end. Anything associated with Nixon has to die. There are wars all over and there will be conflict till the end of time," reveals Carter. "So now what?" asks Murray Smith. "We will change up and make a comeback," states Carter.

As the men get up to leave, Cecil Thomas walks over to Carter.

"Hey, this envelope was left for you," remarks Thomas as he hands Carter the envelope.

Carter opens the envelope. There is a note inside that reads. "Hello Mr. Carter, I think it is time we meet. You have an interesting group of

8MEN. Let's meet at the Bavarian Café in Baltimore. Bring your appetite-Kahn."

Carter storms out.

# BAVARIAN CAFÉ

Former CIA Director Wesley Carter has traveled to the Highlandtown area in Baltimore, Maryland. The note that was left for Carter has piqued his interest. Carter wonders who would have left the note and more importantly who knew about the 8MEN's secret lair. The Bavarian Café is the best German Café outside of Berlin, Germany. Americans rave about the café's authentic dishes. The Bavarian Cafe has been owned by the Kuntz family since the family patriarch Wilhelm immigrated from Germany during the Franco-Prussian War. After passing through Ellis Island, Wilhelm migrated to Baltimore, Maryland.

Fritz Kahn is sitting at a table in the middle of the café. The café only has two other patrons. Kahn has begun his lunch, without Carter. He has ordered potato soup, bratwurst and red cabbage. Carter walks into the somewhat emptied café. He walks over to Kahn's table and throws the note Kahn left for him on the table.

"What the hell is this?" asks Carter.

"Mr. Carter, please have a seat," says Kahn as he motions for Carter to sit down.

"Who the hell are you and what do you want?" asks Carter.

"Mr. Carter, please?" asks Kahn as Carter decides to sit down.

"Ok. I am here. What do you want and who are you?" demands Carter.

"Mr. Carter, please relax," suggests Kahn as he motions to the waiter.

"Yes sir. What can I get you?" asks the waiter.

"I don't want anything," replies an intense Carter as he stares at Kahn.

"Mr. Carter, please order something we have a few things to discuss," says Kahn.

"I'll take a coffee, sugar, and cream," says Carter to the waiter. "So now, why am I here?" he asks Kahn.

"I see that you have left your job. I wanted to present you with an opportunity," mentions a coy Kahn.

"I am retired. I don't want any opportunity from anyone." admits Carter.

"Mr. Carter, no need to be so upset. We are both in the information business. We both want an orderly and peaceful world," declares Kahn.

"I do want a peaceful world, but I want a safe America first and foremost. I don't think that you necessarily want that," hints Carter.

"Mr. Carter, that was impressive. I do want a safe world which of course would include America. But please don't patronize me, you want a safe America under your control. We want a safe world under our control. We are not that much different; we want the same things." concedes Kahn.

"I don't think we want the same things. Your group basically wants to enslave the world to your way of thinking," declares Carter.

"And you use your influence and position to make things happen as you see fit. Mr. Carter there really is no difference. My group has done this for centuries. Your group is just starting out, my group has just perfected it. We want to join forces with your organization. In the end we all want One World Order," claims Kahn.

Carter scoffs at Kahn's assertion that both groups share the same world view.

"How can we want the same thing that you want. Your group was in bed with Hitler. You and your group allowed Hitler to march across Europe. Your group helped make the back room deals that secured the treaties that allowed Hitler to grab the Rhineland and Poland without a fight," conveys an angry Carter.

"Mr. Carter, I must admit you are correct. We thought we could coral Hitler, we were wrong. But we always would rather capitulate than to advocate for war," admits a defeated Kahn.

"And I am supposed to be in league with the people that unleashed Hitler?" rhetorically asks Carter as he gets up to leave.

"Mr. Carter, we can admit our hypocrisy. Can you admit yours?" asks Kahn as Carter is walking away.

"What the hell are you talking about?" questions Carter.

"You criticize me and my organization for our past mistakes. Are you willing to atone for yours? It is not becoming of you to sit on your mountain of morality when in actuality, you wade in the same mud with the rest of us sinners," Carter expresses to Kahn.

"What the…" Carter is interrupted by Kahn.

"What do I mean? We were in league with Hitler before his atrocities. You, your country and your cabal were and are still in league with his foot soldiers that ravished four continents."

Both men take a drink to defuse the tension.

"Again, what do you want from me?" demands Carter.

# THE TOUR

Baltimore City like much of America's metropolitan areas in the United States is still in ruins after the 1968 riots. Unlike Washington, Baltimore's neighbor 30 miles to the south, the "Charm City" has not formulated a plan to revitalize the city in the wake of its destruction. The rampant crime, the increased drug usage and the flight of the city's white population have sped up the city's decay and left it in financial straits.

Wesley Carter and Fritz Kahn are driving in Baltimore looking at the diversity of the city. The drive exposes the poverty and crime-riddled areas of Cherry Hill and Edmondson Village. The drive also shows the seemly tranquil areas of Fells Point, Little Italy, and Greektown.

"America is having some of the same problems Europe had before World War II. After World War I, everyone believed the world was free…that we were all equal. That was a lie in Europe. And that is a lie here. There is always a ruling class. We are a part of that class. The common man cannot be trusted with making certain decisions," suggests Kahn.

"So, you would have a world where the common man has no say so," probes Carter.

"Not to that extreme but the will of the people will cause anarchy," claims Kahn.

"Anarchy?" shouts back Carter.

"Oh yes anarchy, your country is in the midst of it right now. I think the institution of slavery was abhorrent. As well as the practice of your Jim Crow laws, but that was the way you dealt with your Negroes. The Negroes have been an underclass in America for centuries, now they have rights and are gaining more by the day," discloses Kahn.

"So, Negroes gaining rights was a bad thing?" asks Carter.

"Absolutely not, but now your country has to deal with the consequences of their perceived frustration," alleges Kahn.

The men drive by the burned-out shell of the once Baltimore staple, Lexington Market. The Lexington Market was once a bustling commerce center for Baltimoreans of all races and economic levels.

"Here is the outcome of their frustration," affirms Kahn as he points to the north entrance of the market.

"What does this have to do with anything?" challenges a frustrated Carter.

"Americans, you all are so short sighted. We must start to eliminate the forces that don't believe in our values. We must limit the influence of such people throughout the world," states a flippant Kahn.

"Get rid of...you want to get rid of Negroes?" asks Carter.

"No, not as a whole. I have grown rather fond of Michael Jackson and the other Motown folks. Oh, and the Negroes that play in your professional basketball and football leagues. But the Negroes who engage in drugs, who commit crime and those who overpopulate, they all can go. We would be doing humanity a favor," implies Kahn.

"You want to exterminate a race of people. Sorry I can't be involved in that. One holocaust a century," replies Carter.

"Mr. Carter, again it would not be the entire race and it wouldn't only be Negroes." asserts Kahn.

"Well, who else are you talking about?" asks Carter.

"We are really talking about undesirables. The way I see it, the way my group sees it, there are just more Negro undesirables, but I think sexual deviants, homosexuals, the disabled and criminals of all races should go. We need to have a more refined and orderly society," admits Kahn.

"How do you accomplish the craziness you are speaking of?" asks Carter.

"Mr. Carter you already have a vehicle. You just have to go and get it," reveals a devilishly smiling Kahn.

# THE FEAR

Former Director Carter and Fritz Kahn are driving on the Baltimore-Washington Parkway en route to Baltimore-Washington International airport. Kahn is catching a flight to Paris. Carter is consumed in his thoughts about the possibility of knowingly killing Americans on American soil. Carter has been a solider and a politician for more than 30 years, but he has always been a patriot. The thought of killing Americans has Carter feeling like a traitor. Kahn looks at Carter as he seems to be a million miles away.

"I take it this is a decision you can't make," suggests Kahn.

"You mean my decision not to participate in the genocide of American citizens?" replies Carter.

"I see you more as kin to Benjamin Franklin, Thomas Jefferson, Josiah Bartlett, and John Hancock. The patriots that signed your Declaration of Independence. Remember they were subjects of England; they would have been branded traitors had things gone another way," claims Kahn.

Carter scoffs at Kahn's thought.

"Where is my Declaration of Independence. I will end up in a prison in Leavenworth if not hung in some town square for conspiring with foreigners to kill Americans." declares Carter.

"You will be saving your country from a cancer," responds Kahn.

"A cancer?" asks a surprised Carter.

"Yes, a cancer. You have a race of people in your country that you and your forefathers have literally destroyed. How can you trust them? Their hate has been brewing for centuries right under your noses," implies Kahn.

"What are you talking about?" asks Carter.

"Are you white Americans so blind? The Negroes have to hate you. Just think about what you have done to them. Hell, the Jewish Holocaust was a great crime against humanity but what has happened to the Negroes is exponentially worse," alleges Kahn.

"Wait a minute are you saying slavery was worse than what Hitler did?" asks Carter.

"Absolutely, America was 10 or 20 times worse. Hitler destroyed what? Three generations of people with the murder of the Jews. America has destroyed hundreds of generations right here. The American Negroes have been brutalized like no other group in world history. I understand, it is hard to admit the horrible acts. If you admit to the horrible acts, then you have to admit your grandfathers and great-grandfathers were terrible men." suggests Kahn.

"I didn't..." says a stammering Carter.

"Of course, you didn't realize it, your schools don't teach this. The centuries of raping men and women. The senseless murders of babies. I read that poachers in the Louisiana Bayou region used Negro babies as alligator bait. Brutal treatment and all out destruction of these people is hard to fathom. But at some point, America must think that those people are going to want retribution. The thought of their mistreatment is just not going to go away. And your country won't own up to it," declares Kahn.

# EUGENICS

The study of Eugenics delves into the possibility of improving the human race. This study has also investigated improving society by encouraging reproduction by people of positive traits. The original intent of Eugenics has been perverted since its inception in the late 1800s. The Eugenics movement in America was more involved with getting rid of America's deplorables and the unwanted. It has been no coincidence that the Eugenics movement has been run by affluent Americans.

The Eugenics Society of America has been the leading advocates of the movement. The group's agenda was fueled by the thought that America needed to be great again, white men were feeling like they were losing their collective grip on the culture. The past decade has seen the moderate liberation of America's perceived underclasses. The progress of the emerging Black and homosexual populations was going to lay waste to America's white Judeo-Christian values it was thought.

Fritz Kahn instructed Wesley Carter to go the National Institutes of Health in Bethesda, Maryland and retrieve the research and test vials for the Krause virus. The many years Wesley Carter worked as the CIA director afforded him certain clearances that other government employees didn't have. Directors of the intelligence agencies were able to retain their top-secret clearances and their government badges that pretty much allowed entrance into any government building. The NIH is not a heavily secured building. They have one guard in the front of the building with another officer outside in car. Carter walks to the guard at the front desk. The security guard doesn't recognize the Director.

"Identification?" asks the security guard.

Carter reaches in his pocket to pull out his identification.

"Here you go," utters Carter.

The guard looks at the identification and recognizes the Director.

"Director Carter," affirms the excited guard.

Carter looks around hoping no one else recognizes him.

"What can I do for you?" asks the security guard.

Director Carter leans over the guard desk so that no one could hear his request.

"I need access to the storage room in the basement. There are some files that I need to see," divulges Carter.

The security guard walks Director Carter to the basement. The security guard was unaware of the number of national secrets in this single space. The space housed a strand of the Ebola virus, the test strand of the Syphilis virus which was instrumental in the Tuskegee Experiment. But Carter was there to find the research done by German Scientist Albrecht Krause. At the time of his death, Krause had made a breakthrough with autoimmune viruses. Krause's intent was to rid Europe of its Jewish problems. Carter was now contemplating allowing the Lumiere to use the virus to control the Black and gay populations. Was Carter willing to unleash a virus the Nazis could have only dreamt of?

# MASTER PLAN

The direction of the 8MEN was originally plotted by Senator Hampton Capers and former Director of the CIA Wesley Carter. After Senator Capers death, FBI icon J. Edgar Hoover tried unsuccessfully to take over the 8MEN'S global direction. Now Fritz Kahn is jockeying to put his fingerprints on the American Cabal. Kahn wants to use the 8MEN's intelligence and business connections to further the Lumiere's global reach. Since the end of World War II, the United States has become the center of the financial and militaristic strength in the world. Kahn wanted to meet with a few members of the 8MEN in order to start to move his plan forward. The men including Khan, Carter, Murray Smith and Maximillian Love all board an Amtrak train destined for New York City. The gents trek north on the fabled Northeast corridor rail line. The financially strapped rail line has recently been revived by the Amtrak consortium. Fritz Kahn wanted to meet with a few members of the 8MEN without the possibility of any interruptions. The members of the 8MEN and Khan's entourage left Washington, D.C.'s Union Station 30 minutes ago. There hasn't been much talking. Murray Smith has been reading a file while Kahn marvels at the landscape.

"This is a great way to see America. You see the good and bad within a matter of moments. I love the contrast," remarks Kahn.

Murray Smith closes the file and slides it toward Khan.

"Is this thing a joke?" suggests Smith to Khan.

"Did you see this? Are you ok with this?" Smith asks Wesley Carter.

Carter gives a defeated shrug.

"Mr. Smith, what exactly bothers you?" inquires Kahn.

"This whole goddamn thing bothers me. This amounts to genocide," declares Smith.

"Mr. Smith, you sit on a hypocritical perch. Where were you when the 35th President was murdered or when the Civil Rights icon was murdered? Or better yet when the murderers of hundreds of thousands of Jews came to the U.S.? Where were you? I will tell you. You sat there with blood on your hands," implies Khan.

"Those were individuals. You are talking about getting rid of Blacks and homosexuals as a whole," replies Smith.

Wesley Carter listens to the banter between Murray Smith and Fritz Khan but is paralyzed to say anything.

"These measures will only get rid of the weak," declares Khan.

"We can't be a part of this," recites Smith.

Khan looks at Wesley Carter.

"Does he speak for you?" asks Khan of Wesley.

In Wesley Carter's mind he wholeheartedly agrees with Murray Smith, but he doesn't find the words. "What the hell Wesley? You can't go along with this," pleads Smith.

Carter is still speechless.

"Mr. Smith, you are not with us?" asks Kahn.

"Hell no," affirms an angry Murray Smith.

Fritz Kahn signals one of the men in his entourage. The large man grabs Smith from behind the chair by his neck. He is gasping for air as the large man drags him to another train car.

"We can't afford any further interference. We need to move forward," asserts Kahn.

Carter jumps to his feet.

"You need him. How are you going to bypass his media reach? Stop this, I will talk to him, we will straighten this out," begs Carter.

At that moment, there is a large bang. Carter and Maximillian Love turn around. They see the bloodied body of Murray Smith. The large man picks up the body and throws a lifeless Smith into the passing river. Carter and Maximillian Love are in shock. Carter exclaims, "WHAT THE FUCK!"

A calm Kahn declares, "progress Mr. Carter, progress. We must all move forward."

# FAKE NEWS

The death of media mogul Murray Smith reverberated throughout the country. Even though Smith set up a succession plan for his media empire, nobody thought the spry 70-something year-old man would retire anytime soon, but his reported suicide has taken the country by storm. Murray Smith, formerly known as Eithan Murray Smithburg, has been a media icon since coming to the United States shortly before the Nazis sacked Germany in the mid-1930s. Smith recently purchased several mid-sized newspapers in the Midwest and the Southeastern United States. Smith's next venture was to purchase television stations in the top 10 media markets of America. He wanted to bring his brand of journalism into America's living rooms. It has been four days since Murray Smith's alleged suicide, his death is still being investigated. Unfortunately, Smith's body was so disfigured that at this point it has been hard to determine a true cause of death. Funeral services are being finalized by Smith's son Joel. Joel was always going to be Murray's successor. The 32-year-old Joel is trying to come to grips with the death of his father. Wesley Carter has traveled to the Midtown Manhattan headquarters of Smith Media Holdings to help the young Smith cope with his father's death. Wesley Carter has been a sort of Godfather to Joel Smith. Carter has helped Joel out of several scrapes in the past while Murray was out of the country or unable to solve the situation. Joel needed to know what happened to his father and he knew his godfather would probably have the answers. Carter greeted Joel with a hug and kiss on the cheek.

"How are you doing?" asks Carter.

"Still in disbelief. Dad was so full of life. I just can't believe it. He jumps from a train. Something doesn't feel right," hints Joel as a tear rolls down his face.

"Your dad was a great man. Don't you ever forget that," mentions a reassuring Wesley Carter.

"Uncle Wes, how does a man that successful and powerful just kill himself? It is not adding up," implies Joel.

"Joel, it is going to be hard but you're going to have to move on. That's what your father would have wanted.

"I feel like I'm missing something, Uncle Wes."

Carter has a feeling of shame in the pit of his stomach. Joel is asking what happened to his father and Carter knows but he can't tell Joel. Carter knows that if he tells Joel what really happened, he could lose his life also.

Carter decides to pacify Joel. "Your father was a very successful man. The pressures he may have felt, may have overwhelmed him," says Carter. "Uncle Wes, I gotta know," utters a distraught Joel. "Joel, bury your father and then run his company the way he wanted you to. Don't become obsessed with his death, celebrate his life. The truth doesn't always set you free," suggests a rigid Carter.

# MERIDA

The city of Merida sits in Mexico's Yucatan Peninsula. The picturesque city is hours away from the grimy and violent areas most associated with the drug culture of Mexico. Merida is three hours from the burgeoning tourist area of Cancun. It is the home base for the Mexican drug lord Micquel Rojas. The Rojas drug organization has been running the drug trade in Mexico for a little over 10 years. In a move out of mafia lore, Rojas assassinated all the heads of the rival drug families throughout Mexico in one night. The legendary night is referred to as "noche las muertes impias," the night of the unholy deaths. The consequential night sent a fear through Mexico, but it also took away the everyday freedom of Micquel Rojas. He knows one day some new hot shot will come for him. The Rojas organization has run out of market growth, all of Mexico is under Rojas' rule. Rojas has made small inroads into America, but the organization is ready to take the big step to be America's primary drug supplier. Fritz Kahn and Richard Teed have made the trip to Mexico.

The men have enjoyed a silent ride since touching down at the small airport outside of Cancun.

"This is your first time in Mexico?" asks Kahn.

"Yes," utters Teed.

"Not too talkative. Not wondering why we are here?" asks Kahn.

"Doesn't really matter," replies Teed.

The men pull up to the Rojas compound. There is a large security presence outside of the renovated Mayan temple. Micquel Rojas meets Teed and Kahn outside their car. The men walk to the Rojas pool house.

"This is quite a beautiful home," mentions a dotting Kahn.

"Thank you. It took so much time. I think it turned out pretty good," remarks Rojas as he chuckles.

The men walk into the pool house. Rojas signals to his staff to show their guests some hospitality.

"Please have a seat. Can I get you something?" asks Rojas.

"Water is fine," responds Kahn.

"And your associate?" asks Rojas.

"Nothing for me," says Teed.

"I appreciate you coming to Merida. What can I do for you?" asks Rojas.

"I came here to see if there is anything I can do for you," responds Kahn.

"I need to get into the American markets. Can you do something about that?" asks Rojas.

"I am a part of a group in the U.S. that can possibly help you with your problems," alleges Kahn as Teed gives him a death stare.

"You can help me?" challenges Rojas.

"Understand, we are going to want a lot of pesos," asserts a laughing Kahn.

"Money is not a problem. How are you going to smooth over my organization selling drugs in America? I'm pretty sure people in the group will have an issue," remarks Rojas.

"If money is truly not a problem, then it will not be an issue with us. After all, money rules America in the end," says Kahn.

# THE TAKEOVER

The 8MEN have not communicated since Murray Smith's funeral. The group has gathered at its Northeast Washington hideaway. There is an uneasy quiet in the room. The remaining 8MEN are awaiting the arrival of their new member Fritz Kahn. The meeting was supposed to begin at 2 pm. It is now 2:20 pm.

"What the hell?" asks Valerius Torrantio as he looks at his watch.

"He said he would be here," replies Carter.

"I have things I need to do," mentions an impatient Maximilian Love as he begins to walk.

"Gentlemen. Good afternoon, I apologize for my tardiness," states Kahn as he is interrupted by Valerius Torrantio.

"Why is he here?" asks Valerius.

Torrantio is taken aback by the presence of Micquel Rojas. The Rojas organization has been trying to break into the American drug market for years without much success. Noticing the stress on Torrantio's face, Rojas begins to back out of the room.

"Hey, I don't want to start any trouble," says Micquel Rojas.

"Carter, what the hell is going on here?" asks an incensed Valerius Torrantio.

"Mr. Torrantio, please excuse my arrogance. I invited Mr. Rojas here. Mr. Carter had absolutely no idea," admits Kahn with a slight chuckle.

"Do you all know what he does?" asks Valerius with a judgmental tone.

"Mr. Torrantio, Mr. Rojas' organization participates in many of the same vices as the consortium you head," rebuts Kahn.

"Why did you bring him Kahn?" asks a suspicious Carter.

"I apologize for not getting your permission," states Kahn as he is interrupted.

"You were just invited, and you invited someone else, "asserts Valerius.

"I invited Mr. Rojas because I believe he can fill a financial void left by Daniel Bowen. And with the ending of the Vietnam War, there should be some money to fill that hole," implies Kahn.

"You have my attention," admits Maximilian Love. "Mr. Rojas wants safe harbor to enter the American drug trade. He wants to pay this group handsomely for its protection," claims Kahn.

"Are you guys really fucking considering this?" challenges an upset Torrantio.

"Mr. Torrantio, Mr. Rojas didn't want to ruffle any feathers. He is willing to sell to you and your organization at a deep discount," reveals Kahn.

"How deep?" inquires a curious Torrantio. "Thirty percent off of bulk," alleges Kahn.

"Thirty percent, that is not a bad price," admits Torrantio.

"In exchange for what?" asks Carter.

"The protection from your government is needed," responds Rojas.

"We no longer have government control of anything," concedes Carter.

Kahn retorts, "Yes, but former Director Carter your word still carries weight. The right word to the right people, and if needed, the right amount of money to the right official goes a long way. America is always for sale, right?"

Valerius Torrantio is upset by the impending inclusion of Micquel Rojas into the 8MEN.

# THE RUSE

Richard Teed has been an associate of the 8MEN for the past 25 years. Even though Teed has not always agreed with the group, he normally understood their end goal. Former Director Wesley Carter and the late Hampton Capers preached the adage of the "Patriotic Capitalist." Following this line of thinking, Teed understood the group's foray into the Vietnam War. The war was profitable for the organization and helped the U.S. to get a military foothold in Eastern Asia. Teed was not happy with the assassinations of President Kennedy and Dr. King, but he could make sense of their deaths being for the greater good of the country to ease tensions. But Teed cannot find the rationale for the group to jump into the illegal drug business and allow the death of one of its charter members. As Teed saw it, the 8MEN are bringing a cancer to the doorsteps of Americans. There is absolutely nothing patriotic about that. He felt he needed to talk to Carter, and it just couldn't wait. Teed got in touch with Carter and asked him to meet him at the Ellipse outside the White House.

Carter was always an admirer of the picturesque Ellipse, especially on an early fall day. Carter is sitting on a park bench soaking in all the Americana going on around him. On days like this, Carter believes all his deal making and backroom conniving was worth it. If a father can safely throw a baseball around with his son on a Saturday, then he has done his job.

"Plotting your comeback?" asks Teed he sits down next to Carter.

"Not at all. I don't think the new resident would want any parts of my politics," claims Carter as both men look toward the White House.

"Yeah, he seems to be a good man," jabs Teed.

"The peanut farmer. He is over his head. That job isn't really for a good man. The power is consuming. You didn't ask me here to debate politics with me. It sounded serious," snaps Carter.

"I'm trying to figure out what is going on. You gave up control of the 8MEN to a crazy man," said Teed.

"Maybe I just needed to step back and put some distance between things after Watergate," unconvincingly says Carter.

Teed condescendingly responds," are you going to tell me the truth?"

Carter takes a deep breath before saying, "I wanted to protect you all. I have been trying to figure out a way to get rid of Kahn."

"Get rid of?" questions Teed.

Carter looks around to make sure no one is listening before he starts to speak. "Kahn has a file with many of the things that the 8MEN conspired. In the file he notes how the Vietnam War was started. He has very detailed information about the assassinations. I'm in there… you and Danya are also. He has the slush fund information where we paid the Italian hitmen. He has it all. He has a fucking roadmap to bring us all down," says a defeated Carter.

"So, we just continue to do whatever he wants?" demands Teed.

"Do you have a better plan?" asks Carter.

"No, but he seems to be devising plans to destabilize America. And we have got to stop that, right?" asks Teed.

His question seems to have awakened the dormant patriotic spirit in Carter.

"You are right. We do need to stop this. I don't know when, but I am going to need you to find that file," says Carter.

# THE SNITCH

American politics has always been a blood sport. But the 1970s have taken the perceived games of politics to a new level. Scandal and upheaval are at an all-time high. The Watergate scandal has awakened the American public's collective mind to the evils performed by the American Government's sworn servants. Americans have always thought their government officials were good at their core, but the actions of the Nixon administration made the public think, "what else was out there?" Many in the news business were caught flat-footed with this scandal. Journalists were always thought of as the fourth branch of government, the media was nonexistent during much of Watergate. It was thought by its critics, that the media was a little too cozy with politicians to get an accurate picture of what was truly going on. After the kudos received by The Post's Carl Bernstein and Bob Woodward, a more "in-your-face" journalism has been born. Watergate opened the flood gates for investigative journalism. Every so-called reporter wants to be the next Woodward or Bernstein. Washington is fraught with rumors of additional scandals that weren't uncovered during the Nixon take down. Steven Whitmer was a beat reporter for the New York Times. Whitmer was awarded the Pulitzer Prize in 1973 for his expose' on the New York mob's strangle hold on the garbage industry. There were a rash of waste management company owners who were killed or gravely injured. The spotlight Whitmer shined forced New York City and New York State to pay attention to their awarded garbage contracts. The expose' led to the prosecution of several low-level mafia soldiers. The regional attention started to raise the national profile of the prized writer. Whitmer has aspirations of being a national television correspondent. He decides to go to Washington to follow up on some murmurs from inside sources. Whitmer is given a tip about a possible story on several political assassinations. His curiosity is piqued. Whitmer has set a meeting at his go to Bistro, "Blanche's All-American" located in Hell's Kitchen. Whitmer brought several of his mob confidential sources to the restaurant after the meals they normally spilled their guts. He thought the diminutive black lady from Calvert County, Maryland brought him good luck. So, he decided to try his luck again. Whitmer meets with a low-level Saudi national named Mahmood Azaim. Azaim moved to Washington after graduating from Columbia University to take a job at the Saudi consulate. Azaim was a fan of Whitmer's work in New York. The men meet at Blanche's All-American, as Whitmer walks into the restaurant immediately spotting Mahmood in the somewhat empty establishment. The men shake hands as Whitmer sits down.

"How are you?" asks Whitmer.

"I am good," responds Mahmood.

Whitmer looks at a menu.

"What's good here?" asks Whitmer.

"The beer," replies Mahmood.

"Easy enough," agrees Whitmer as he puts away the menu.

Mahmood slides Whitmer an envelope across the table. Whitmer opens the envelope and takes the papers out. Whitmer's eyes open wide.

"Are you shitting me? Where the hell did you get this," inquires Whitmer.

"The Saudi government has been sitting on this information for years, but the story needs to get out," discloses Mahmood.

"Of course, I need to verify, but shit. The Mob is in bed with the CIA and Mossad. I'm going to get another fucking Pulitzer award behind this one," hints a gleeful Whitmer.

# EASTER EGG HUNT

New York City's Central Park hosts an annual easter egg hunt. The event brings together kids from all over the city to enjoy the season. Teed and Danya decided to bring Keleeha to this year's hunt. Keleeha is having a ball playing with complete strangers. Danya dotes from a distance; she can't be happier to see Keleeha laughing and having a good time. Danya looks back at Teed with an angelic smile. Teed has a self-satisfying smile on his face witnessing his happy family. Teed couldn't be more at peace.

"This is a beautiful scene," states Director Carter as he sits down next to Teed on a nearby park bench. "How can you destroy such a beautiful day," replies Teed.

"Teed, I am hurt," claims Carter.

"What do you want?" asks Teed.

"I need you to assist with a mission," responds Carter.

"A mission? I thought the 8MEN were done?" asks Teed.

"We have been reborn young man," replies Carter "What is the pay?" asks Teed.

"Don't you worry, you will be well compensated," states Carter.

"So. What is the job?" asks Teed.

"We will meet in the next week to bring you up to speed," discloses Carter as he stands.

The men shake hands.

"Go enjoy your family," recites Carter as he walks away.

Teed walks over to Danya.

"What did he want?" asks an irritable Danya.

Teed gives Danya a hug.

"He wants me to help with a mission. She is really having a good time," conveys Teed as he watches Keleeha prance around.

"She really is," admits a smiling Danya.

Keleeha runs over to Danya and Teed.

"Mommy, my arm is hurting," states Keleeha as she winces from pain.

"Honey, did you hit something?" queries Danya.

"No," says Keleeha as the pain becomes more evident.

"We have got to get her a hospital," says a concerned Danya.

They all rush out of the park to find a cab.

# MOUNT SINAI

Danya Franck's family and other prominent Jewish families from Europe gifted millions of dollars to Mount Sinai hospital pre-World War II. Mount Sinai along with Mercy Hospital in Cincinnati were the only hospitals in America that would openly treat Jewish Americans in the early 20th century. Mount Sinai has built an excellent reputation and has transitioned into one of the top teaching hospitals in the country. Not too far from Central Park, Danya and Teed requested that their Yellow Cab driver take their ailing daughter to Mount Sinai. The agony is apparent on Keleeha's sweaty face and through the groans from the pain as they hit each bump. The pains have gone from her arms to now including pain in her back and legs. As the family arrives at the hospital, Teed picks up his pain riddled child and runs into the emergency room. Teed makes a beeline straight for the nurse's desk.

"My daughter, we don't know what is wrong," remarks Teed.

Noticing the pain that Keleeha is in, the nurse jumps up and leads Teed to an area where patients are seen. Teed lays Keleeha on a bed.

"Daddy, it hurts," affirms Keleeha. Teed hugs his child trying to soothe away her pain. Hours later Dr. Mendelssohn visited the sleeping Keleeha.

"I see she is sleeping," whispers Dr. Mendelssohn.

"She has had a rough day," responds Teed.

"We should step into the hallway. Let her get her rest," suggests Dr. Mendelssohn as he leads Danya and Teed to the hallway to talk.

"We got back the results of Danya's test. She has been diagnosed with Sickle Cell Anemia," discloses Dr. Mendelssohn.

"What is that?" questions Teed.

"Sickle Cell Anemia is a hereditary blood disorder that affects the blood flow. Your daughter has a special type of blood that does not carry oxygen well. Because of the lack of oxygen, a normal rounded cell could form a sickled shape.

Danya begins to cry as the gravity of Keleeha's condition sets in.

"So, what will that do to Keleeha?" asks Teed.

"The red blood cells in her blood vessels will not flow freely. This will prevent her vital organs from getting the necessary oxygen. She will tire very easily and feel weak," asserts Dr. Mendelsohn.

"Is there a treatment?" asks Danya.

"Yes, we can treat her," says Dr. Mendelsohn.

Danya momentarily feels relief.

"We will do whatever we need to do for her," proclaims Teed with a fatherly tone.

# UNCONDITIONAL

Since learning about Keleeha's medical condition, Teed and Danya, her adopted parents, have become a portrait of unconditional love. The couple are now full-time caretakers, tending to every want and need of their child. Thankfully, Keleeha has not experienced any major Sickle Cell flair ups in the past year. Danya and Teed have enrolled Keleeha in Whitaker Day School. The Upper Westside school boasts that its parents contribute millions of dollars annually to civic causes and volunteer thousands of hours to city initiatives, implying that the families of the school are willing to give of their time and money. The Whitaker Day School has a lengthy waiting list, but with the right donation, slots seem to open up. An anonymous $20,000 donation for the school's Capital Campaign was received in the name of Keleeha Teed. Within days, Keleeha gained acceptance into the school's first grade. She has adjusted well to the new school. For the most part, Keleeha has fit in with most of her classmates. However, there are a few students who are not fans of the new kid. Even the first grade at Whitaker Day School has a hierarchy. The first-grade elementary school politics are ruled by Kasey Winthrop. Kasey has been less than happy with the attention Keleeha has been receiving. Kasey decides to approach Keleeha on the playground. Keleeha is sitting on a park bench reading Charlotte's Web. She seems captivated by the literary classic judging by her facial expression as she reads. Kasey and two other mean girls walk over to the unsuspecting Keleeha.

"What's your name?" asks Kasey.

Keleeha looks up from her book.

"My name is Keleeha," Kasey and the two mean girls start to laugh.

"Keleeha, that's a funny sounding name," replies Kasey.

"Sounds like a dog's name," suggests Amy as the girls start to laugh.

"And look, she's reading Charlotte's Web. Such a baby's book," alleges Kasey as Keleeha gets up and walks away in tears.

Later in the afternoon, Danya is walking up to the school. She overhears a conversation with Kasey's mother talking to a couple of other mothers.

"Their class was set for the year. They have some new girl in their class, her name is Keleeha. I don't think she is going to fit in. With a name like Keleeha, she won't be coming to any of Kasey's birthdays," claims Lisbeth Winthrop as she and the other mothers start to laugh.

A short time later, Danya and Keleeha are walking holding hands walking down West 57th Street.

"So, how was school?" asks Danya.

"Ok I guess," replies Keleeha.

"Just ok," interrogates Danya.

"Do I have to stay at this school? I don't think the kids like me," reveals a sad Keleeha.

Danya had hoped that Keleeha was unaware of the mean spiritedness directed toward her. Danya bends down to look Keleeha in the eye.

"Give me two weeks, and if you still want to leave, then that will be fine. Is that okay?" asks Danya as she gives Keleeha a big hug.

Danya thinks to herself how she can resolve this situation.

# MAMA BEAR

The protection of a parent's child is innate to most human beings. Danya did not give birth to Keleeha but the love she feels for her rivals the aggression of a mama bear defending her cubs. She is not going to allow her daughter to be bullied and most certainly will not allow anyone to question her worthiness.

Danya has been studying the schedule of Lisbeth Winthrop over the last week. She has been stalking the unsuspecting mother like she was big game. It hurt Danya to her heart that this woman and her band of aging mean girls allowed their mean children to intimidate Keleeha. It was Danya's intention to speak to the woman and appeal to her better nature. But she really hoped it went another way. Lisbeth Winthrop is going about her day in a normal fashion. The Upper Westside socialite is consumed with planning the annual "Every Child" fashion show fundraiser. The event raises money to send so-called underprivileged kids to summer camp upstate. Lisbeth loves the event; she gets to hob nob with other Westside socialites and the occasional celebrity who donates to the event. Lisbeth is walking up W. 57th Street with her full attention in the Vogue magazine she has been reading. She is plotting out the movements and the outfits the young teens will wear walking down the runway.

"The crowd will love this," murmurs a giddy Lisbeth as she is abruptly pulled into an alley.

"What the hell? Who are you?" questions Lisbeth with her snooty attitude.

"I am Keleeha's mother," states a somewhat reserved Danya.

"Keleeha, is that the little nig.."

Lisbeth is violently interrupted by Danya. She pins her to the wall with the bottom of her heeled boot.

"Now, that I have your attention. You will make sure your daughter and her friends will no longer bully my child," demands as Lisbeth's eyes bulge from the fear.

Lisbeth tries to speak but Danya's boot is restricting her from breathing. Danya loosens her grip.

"Speak, calmly," instructs Danya.

"My little Kasey couldn't hurt a fly," pleads Lisbeth.

"Your little Kasey torments my Keleeha daily," claims Danya as her anger increases.

As Danya's anger increases, she puts more pressure on Lisbeth's throat. Lisbeth starts to gasp for air. Danya realizes that she can't continue. She releases Lisbeth as she falls to the ground.

"I am sorry. This will never happen again if my child stays safe," whispers Danya as she walks out of the alley.

# THE FATHERLAND

Gesundheit was the brainchild of Maximilian Love. Maximilian came to the United States as a part of the Paperclip program back in the late-40s. Unlike many of the former Nazis, Maximilian decided to change his name upon coming to America. The former Gunther Braun was like German royalty. Although not directly related to the Fuhrer, Gunther was the second cousin of Hitler's rumored wife Eva Braun. Gunther's father, Baron, was a leading scientist and the creator of several biological weapons in development at the time of his death in 1943. Following in his father's footsteps, it was natural for Gunther to continue his father's research. Baron Braun worked on all types of biological weapons. He once developed malaria- carrying mosquitoes that would be deployed against an enemy in order to sicken the population before an invasion. The mosquitoes were meant for the planned invasion of America. Even though many of the weapons were never used outside of testing, the discovery of the weapons and the associated research was a militaristic bonanza for the Americans who discovered they were far behind the German researchers. The power players in national security knew they had to get the developers on the side of the U.S., or they would be drafted by their bubbling adversary, the Soviet Union. The Pentagon and the State Department gave birth to the Paperclip program. The program allowed Gunther to start a new life as Maximilian Love. As a part of Maximilian's agreement, he was to start a pharmaceutical company that would continue the research and development of the somewhat controversial medical research begun under Nazi rule. During his time with the Reich, Love oversaw the development of many new operational procedures and the creation of many biological weapons. The Nazi regime allowed and encouraged experimentation of new drugs and radical surgeries on their Jewish captives. Fritz Kahn saw Gesundheit as a crucial part of his depopulation efforts. Kahn knew that Gesundheit was instrumental to the controversial Fairhope experiment. The tiny town of Fairhope, Alabama played host to the classified research on the effects of young Black women contracting the sexually transmitted disease Chlamydia. The United States government gave Gesundheit the cover to experiment on the unsuspecting black women of the small Alabama town. The experiment left many young women effected by the disease causing unknown physical complications for the area's Black residents for well over 25 years. Fritz Kahn arrives at Gesundheit to a Presidential rollout, Love has literally rolled out the red carpet.

"Wow, this really is nice but wasn't necessary," comments Kahn as he is surprised by the reception he has received.

"I wanted you to know how important I thought your visit was," suggests Love.

The two men along with their entourages walk through the Gesundheit facility.

"I am very impressed with your company's operation," declares a complimentary Kahn.

"Thank you very much," says Love.

"Have you vetted your employees? The biological materials that will be sent here are of a sensitive nature," Kahn whispers to Love.

"These people know discretion," remarks Love.

"Good, let's move forward," states Kahn as the men continue their tour.

# THE ROOT

The 95th Congress was due to begin in a little over two weeks. But the phenomenon known as Joshua Youngbuck has already taken Washington by storm. Youngbuck' s resentment for the corruption in Washington was refreshing for many. The Senator-Elect has not written one bill or attended one committee meeting. But already the masses are committing their full faith that this neophyte will help resurrect the true values of public service. The Washington Rotary Club is hosting its Biannual prayer breakfast to coincide with the incoming Congress. In most years, this event is covered by the local D.C. papers, but this year much of the national media will cover the event in hopes of getting a great soundbite from Senator-Elect Youngbuck. He is overwhelmed by the large media presence as he begins his speech.

"Wow. Look at this. This is a great turnout," states the plain speaking Youngbuck.

The gathered crowd gives a slight chuckle.

"Ladies and gentlemen, I appreciate you coming out today. Many have wondered why I ran for Congress. My background wasn't politics, nobody in my family was in politics. My parents raised me to be a responsible and trustworthy man. I ran for Congress as an extension of my military service. I wanted to continue to give back. This country has given me...given all of us so much. I decided to run because my beloved America is in crisis. We didn't trust our President or our military leaders. Our military engagement in Vietnam was not ideal. How and why we were there has still not been fully explained to me. Before getting into politics, I thought that it was just me and my brothers in arms and our families that were dealing with pain and loss. But that is not true, most Americans have lost and suffered immeasurable pain because of differing reasons. It is a must that we put the Vietnam War as well as the Watergate disgrace behind us. We need to keep the root of all evil out of our nation's politics. I hope to propose legislation that will limit money in our government on the local and national levels. Our government must work for every man, not just the rich man."

The crowd leaps to their feet with a thunderous applause as he continues. "We must put these horrible things behind us, but never shall we forget. We have seen what happens. We must make sure none of this happens ever again," proclaims a determined Youngbuck.

# SWEARING IN

The new Congress was set to tackle some tough legislation, but they may be constrained by old politics. Many within the Congress wanted to root out the corruption within the government and they wanted to enhance law enforcement efforts throughout the country. Taking on corruption and the bolstering of public safety was a winning strategy. Who could campaign against that? The 1976 election was a bloodbath for Republicans and Democrats saw an opportunity to institute some legislation that could show that they were strong on law enforcement and corruption. Senator Jeffrey Anderson was poised to become the Senate majority leader. The New York Senator has a long career advocating liberal ideals and most notably, was the first white Senator to sign on to the historic Voting Rights Act of 1964. Wesley Carter set up a meeting between Senator Anderson and Fritz Kahn. The men meet at the Mayflower Hotel in a secluded room. Kahn is sitting when Senator Anderson and his security detail enters the room. The men exchange pleasantries.

"Mr. Kahn," said Anderson.

"So, what can I do for you Mr. Fritz?"

"Would you like a drink or something?" asks Kahn.

"No thank you," responds Anderson.

"So, let's get down to business," replies Kahn as he slides an envelope to the Senator.

Senator Anderson takes the papers out of the envelope. It is the framework of legislation.

"This is legislation, isn't it?" asks Anderson.

He starts to read the paperwork and then puts it back in the envelope in disgust.

"It is," affirms Kahn.

"I don't know what this is, but we write our own legislation," states Anderson.

Kahn places a bag of money on the table.

"I didn't think this would be a free favor. Please take a look," requests Kahn.

"There's no need. I'm not going to play that game," declares Anderson.

"I understand. You are a very virtuous man and above corruption. The problem is you are not above it," alleges Kahn as he slides pictures of Anderson and several members of the New York mob dining in midtown Manhattan. Senator Anderson has a look of defeat on his face.

"Take the money and the pictures. The bill will be great for you and your caucus. You will look like a great steward of the American Government," suggests Kahn.

"Once I do this, what do you get?" challenges a puzzled Anderson.

"A safer world," remarks Kahn.

# PAGEANTRY

Senator Youngbuck has shared the pageantry of his swearing in ceremony with his family including his 30-year-old wife Jessica, his five-year-old son Elijah, and his three-year-old daughter Gabrielle. After being sworn in, the newly elected majority leader Jeffrey Anderson had a brief meeting with the new Democratic members. The majority leader gave the new members the lay of the land. He expressed his thanks for their hard work during the campaign, but even more for the work they will soon embark upon. The new Senators greet each other and talk about the day's events. Senator Anderson makes his way over to Senator Youngbuck.

"Senator Youngbuck," states Senator Anderson as he reaches out to shake his hand.

Senator Youngbuck is awestruck to think the liberal icon knows his name.

"Senator Youngbuck, if you have a moment, I would like to speak with you in my office." The gentlemen walk back to Senator Anderson's office.

Senator Youngbuck is amazed by Senator Anderson's office.

"This is impressive," remarks Youngbuck.

"Your office isn't too shabby, either. Joshua, I asked you to come here because I want to get your feelings on strategy for some legislation," proclaims Senator Anderson.

"Anything I can do to help," responds Youngbuck.

"Great, you were great on the trail talking about corruption. Nixon really set us back. It is hard for the American people to trust us," claims Anderson as he slides an envelope to Senator Youngbuck.

"This is a framework of some legislation to try to curb the lack of law enforcement in this country," discloses Anderson.

"Just from a glance this seems to want to build prisons and strengthen laws against drug dealers," questions Youngbuck.

"You are quite perceptive, but on page 2 it spells out how we will address corruption in politics," implies Senator Anderson as Senator Youngbuck flips over the page acknowledging Anderson's claims.

"My apologies," said Youngbuck.

"No problem. I want you to champion this legislation," mentions Anderson.

"Me? Why me?" inquires a surprised Youngbuck.

"You are a symbol of America's good nature. People rallied around you in Michigan. And the nation will now rally behind you to fix this.

Can America count on you, Senator Youngbuck?" requests Anderson.

"Yes, you can," says Youngbuck hesitantly.

# PRISON INC.

The prison system in the United States by many accounts was created to rehabilitate criminals. It was thought that the punishment of medieval Europe was barbaric and cruel. Throughout the history of the United States, the prison system and its philosophies have changed depending on the mindset of the community it was serving. The modern American prison is still charged with rehabilitating the country's worst, but now there is another less described reason for the system. Prisons on all levels have been used to frighten people into fearing the loss of their freedom and to send a message to Americans that they will be safe. The United States prison population is beginning to spike. Much of the uptick is from the rhetoric of politicians on both sides of the political divide. The unrest could make for a future financial windfall that Kahn is looking to exploit. He has begun to put his plans in motion to begin a building boom of the next generation of American prisons. These new-aged prisons would make money through the warehousing of criminals and as a contractor of low-priced labor. Kahn has set a meeting with William Taylor, president of Gefangis, a small private company specializing in detention centers in rural Florida counties and his partner James Stiller. "Gentlemen, I represent a group that wants to get into business with you," recites Kahn.

"Mr. Kahn, I appreciate that you have come to us with this opportunity, but we don't understand what you want from us," inquires William Taylor.

"Gentlemen, I want your infrastructure and your know how," claims Kahn.

"Again Mr. Kahn we don't understand how there would be such a boom in prisons," questions Stiller.

Kahn knows he can't tip his hand about the coming onslaught of drugs to the region. The Rojas organization has been slowly taking over the drug market in South Florida and many metropolitan areas in Louisiana, Alabama, and Georgia. Knowing he is introducing the virus; Kahn readies the cure while making a profit.

"Gentlemen, let's cut to the chase. I want a 51% interest in your company," admits Kahn to Taylor and Stiller.

"We will have to think about it," concedes a bewildered Taylor.

Kahn motions to one of his bodyguards.

"Tell them to bring the bags." Two large men enter the room carrying two large duffle bags. A bag is placed in front of both Taylor and Stiller.

"Go ahead, open them," demands Kahn.

Both men are very apprehensive about opening the bag. They open the bag to find $50,000 in cash.

"This is just a down payment on the $5 million I will pay you both. But I need your answer now," divulges Kahn.

Both men smile with excitement while nodding their heads yes.

# THE TRINITY

The 8MEN are at a crossroads. The group has had a very lucrative partnership throughout the years. Much of the 8MEN's financial windfall came from the cabal's involvement in the Vietnam War. The war's end will surely put a dent in their coffers. They are set to meet to catch up on unfinished business and receive one of their last checks from Cecil Thomas. As the group enters their meeting space in Northwest Washington, they notice Fritz Kahn writing on a chalk board.

"Somebody got to school early today," suggests Cecil Thomas as the group laughs.

Wesley Carter looks at Kahn very suspiciously.

"What is this?" asks Carter.

"I had some thoughts, so I wanted to jot them down," states Kahn as the 8MEN see the blackboard filled with Kahn's rambling notes.

"You had a lot of thoughts," implies Maximilian Love.

"Once I got started, I just kept going. This group's main financial source has been the money made by Mr. Thomas' company from the Vietnam War. As we know, the war has ended. So now what do we do?" asks Kahn as he is interrupted.

"This country is not going to stand for another war," offers Cecil Thomas as Kahn continues.

"No, they aren't but there are some other fruitful activities that we can definitely take advantage of," theorizes Kahn as the group sits at the oval table except Wesley Carter.

Carter goes to the liquor cart and pours himself a glass of scotch.

"Much like you all getting in on the ground floor when it came to the Vietnam War, we are going to get in on the ground floor with these three burgeoning opportunities: drugs, prisons and medical treatment," asserts Kahn as the group looks at him in amazement.

"Do you mean drugs like pharmaceuticals? You know I have a pharmaceutical company," queries a confused Maximilian Love. "Pharmaceuticals are involved in this but the drugs I am referring to are street drugs. The Rojas organization is going to flood the low-income areas of this country with these drugs. Our cut will be 30% off of each shipment," alleges Kahn.

"If you do that, you will destabilize every city in this country," pushes back Carter.

"Mr. Carter you are correct, that's why we need some of those Senators that have been in this group's pocket to introduce legislation calling for more enhanced policing and the construction of more prisons. We are going to need a place to house the low-level drug dealers and the users. This will also help with some of the country's so-called "nigger problems." What the drugs and the prison don't rid us of will be taken care with a virus."

Cecil Thomas interrupts, "What virus, what kind of craziness are you talking about?"

Kahn answers confidently, "Mr. Thomas, I assure there is nothing crazy about this. A virus will be introduced into the colored and gay communities. Two birds, one stone. The virus will devastate both communities. On the back end we will come in with a cure. We will be heroes. Very rich heroes. This will stretch for decades. The money we make from this will pale in comparison to your kickbacks from the Vietnam War," declares Kahn.

# THE BILL

The recent uptick of violent crimes throughout the nation has inspired debate within the U.S. Congress. Senate Bill number 121608 dubbed "Prison Inc." has gained champions from both sides of the Senate aisle, but many liberal members have railed against the legislation. The proponents of the bill believe it would jail those who have a blatant disregard for law and order. Recent violent crimes in Florida and Georgia have spurred an agitation for incarcerating any type of violators. Two high-profile murders in the south seemed to be the final straw. In both cases two suburban white families were robbed and murdered by non-white perpetrators. Many believed the underlying reason for the bill and some of the perceived harsh consequences were racially motivated. The south has seen a surge of drug activity and drug influenced crimes. The bill had come up for debate on the floor of the United States Senate. The Democrats have been placed in a strange position. Neophyte Senator Joshua Youngbuck was sponsoring the controversial bill with Republican Senator Kevin James. The bill has received support from police unions, real estate companies, chambers of commerce and an abundance of civic organizations throughout the country. But there has been pushback from liberal organizations, thinking this law would be used to constitute tougher laws on people of color. The primary congressional opponent is

Maryland Senator Phillip Leake. Senator Leake has large liberal support from Maryland strongholds: Baltimore City and suburban Washington, D.C. counties: Prince George's and Montgomery. Senator Youngbuck has been speaking on the Senate floor for a little over 20 minutes.

"In closing I know this is a tough choice. But we have to protect our families and communicate to the criminals that we all take crime very seriously. The criminals know our laws better than the lawyers that represent them. I am willing to listen to amendments, but we need to pass this law so that we can give law enforcement the backup they need. Thank you for listening," remarks Senator Youngbuck as he receives applause from half of the Senate chamber.

Moments later Senator Leake takes to the floor.

"Good afternoon colleagues. I must commend Senator Youngbuck. He has crafted a bill that has brought together many special interest groups. This bill will be great for businesses, but how about fairness for the least of us? This bill will allow law enforcement a lot of latitude for police intrusion and harsher sentences given out by judges. We must stop this bill in hopes of more equitable policing and sentencing. Thank you." responds Senator Leake.

Senator Youngbuck garnered enough support to pass the measure, but the trick is going to be getting a veto-proof majority. President Jimmy Carter has promised he would veto the bill. Carter owes his election to many of the same Black people who would be affected by this new law. Fritz Kahn has been sitting in the gallery of the Senate watching the democratic process play out. The sense is that the measure will pass but won't see the light of day. New York Senator Anderson sits next to Fritz Kahn.

"The measure will pass, but Carter will surely block it. There are too many bleeding hearts running around here," asserts a defeated Senator Anderson

"Senator Anderson, you must have faith. We just need to find the right circumstances to change the bleeding hearts' minds," suggest a gleeful Kahn.

# FREEBASE

The Rojas organization has been running the drug trade in the southeastern U.S. over the last six months. With the Italian mafia severely crippled, the Rojas organization has begun to creep northward. The nation's capital has always been fertile ground for the drug trade. The city's water access allows for large shipments to covertly arrive, and the endless money fueled by political power makes for a dangerous recipe. The Rojas organization ran its business much like any other pharmaceutical company…without the murdering. They have been testing a cheaper version of cocaine called freebase. Freebase was normally created by mixing cocaine with water and baking soda. This shift will forever change the "highfalutin'" image of cocaine and make it accessible to the unsuspecting poor. In the tests, the Rojas organization has conducted they have noticed certain addictive qualities not noticed in the powdered version. The rich patrons have spent small fortunes on their addictions, but the poor folks have resorted to bartering and criminal acts to satisfy their habits. Micquel Rojas is watching one of the open-air drug markets his underlings have set up along Massachusetts Avenue, a short 5-minute ride to the U.S. Capitol.

"Business seems to be good," says Rojas.

"I think so, but of course the Black guys don't like that we have taken their territory," mentions Luis Sanchez. Sanchez is the Rojas organization's enforcer. He is a part of the strike force that recons each area they look to take over. He made his reputation in the streets of Mexico City and Tijuana. Sanchez scouts each city to find who was the most feared drug dealer and made it a point to kill them and display their bodies for the public to see. Washington, D.C. was no different, reputed drug kingpin Joseph "Joe Joe" Fox was murdered three weeks ago. He was found in his torched Mercedes Benz.

"The money is good. We have people coming back asking for it. Some come back without money," alleges Sanchez.

Rojas and Sanchez notice a man obviously wanting the drug without any money. Sanchez cocks the hammer on his gun and runs to the corner to investigate. Rojas watches from a safe distance. He can't hear what is going but he sees Sanchez confront the man. The man takes a swing at Sanchez. Sanchez ducks the punch and hits the man with an upper cut, knocking the man clear off his feet. Sanchez pulls his gun and points it at the man. There is a whistle from Rojas' car. Rojas motions for Sanchez. He runs over to the car.

"Boss?" asks a panting Sanchez.

"Bring him here," requests Rojas.

"Get him up and bring him," barks Sanchez to his underlings.

The bloodied man stumbles over to the car.

"Sir you are in a situation. You are aware you are about to be killed. Aren't you? But I think I can help you. Are you interested?" inquires Rojas.

The man realizes he has no choice, so he nods his head yes.

# THE PAWN

Lieutenant Colonel Joshua Youngbuck was not used to losing. Even when Youngbuck had a momentary set back, he normally made a course correction, then overcame his hurdle. But none of his setbacks were as public as the defeat of the "Prison Inc." Bill. The media continues to run stories about the freshman senator's resounding defeat. The main narrative seemed to center on the fact that Youngbuck didn't understand the Senate and as a neophyte didn't know his place. He thought that the "Prison Inc." Bill could be something that united members from both sides of the political divide. Youngbuck learned what many first-time policy makers learn: your good idea is the devil's spawn to the other side. The idea of securing America from senseless violence is a uniting thought but the solution is always a fleeting notion. Senator Youngbuck was in an emotional funk. He was questioning why he ever ran for political office. He thought his idea to curb the rising violence in his beloved country would be met with overwhelming approval, but of course that's not what happened. He has been accused of being a Northern Dixiecrat and being in the pocket of an array of special interest groups. All of these notions hurt Youngbuck to his heart. To get over his frustration, Youngbuck searched D.C. for a restaurant that served his guilty pleasure, Detroit style pizza. Only Detroit native, Joseph "Smitty Bear" Smith created the doughy monstrosity. The Detroit pizza packed on the pounds compared to its east coast cousin. Youngbuck traveled to "Smitty Bear's" in Northwest Washington, D.C., to quench his pizza fix. Youngbuck sat in the bistro for little over an hour devouring the assortments of meats and vegetables atop his pizza, it gave him a feeling of Xanadu. But the reality was he still felt like a failure. Youngbuck paid his bill and left his waitress a nice tip. He walked out of the restaurant onto Constitution Avenue just four short blocks from The Capitol. Youngbuck starts to walk toward his apartment on L Street when he is approached by a somewhat nervous Black man.

"Give me your money, man!" demands the robber as he sticks a 22-caliber gun into Youngbuck's back. "Sure thing, I'll give you anything you want," replies Youngbuck.

Youngbuck's military training wasn't going to allow him to be robbed. As he reaches to give the robber his wallet, the nervous man shoots Youngbuck twice in the back. The scared robber runs off. Two police officers along the street give chase. One officer stops to help Youngbuck. He is bleeding profusely and begins to gasp for air. Within a minute, Youngbuck is gone. The police corner the robber in an alley. With no alternatives, the robber drops his gun. The police officers look around to see if there are any witnesses.

"Please, I made a mistake. I didn't mean…"
The officers shoot the burglar four times, killing him instantly.

# THE FALLEN

The murder of Joshua Youngbuck has exponentially heightened the fears of violence many are currently feeling in the country. The brazen attack on the Senator made many think about their own mortality. If a United States Senator could be killed on the streets of Washington, D.C., what chance did the rest of us have? The last three days since Senator Youngbuck's death has been a massive shift for policing, the city of Washington, D.C. and many other cities along the eastern seaboard. These particular regions have decided to show an overwhelming law enforcement presence in the streets. His death has given the law enforcement community the excuse they needed to militarize the country's largest police forces. Senator Youngbuck has laid in state at the U.S. Capitol the last three days. Members of Congress from both sides of the aisle have come to pay their respects to the freshman senator from Michigan. People from all walks of life have come to pay homage, a large contingent from Lieutenant Youngbuck's military troop has come to pay the fallen hero his honor. After the emotional funeral and burial service at Arlington National Cemetery, the Senate has decided to have Senator Youngbuck's widow, Jessica addresses the Congress in prime time to be carried by the three major television networks. Jessica Youngbuck walks into the Senate chamber to thunderous applause. Members from the

Senate and the House rush to give her consoling hugs, it would seem that political views have been placed on the back burner over the last three days. Mrs. Youngbuck makes her way to the podium; she stands there while members of Congress continue to applaud her. Moments later she begins to speak.

"Good evening members of Congress and good evening to the American people watching at home. Today, we celebrated and buried an American hero, my husband Lieutenant First Class Joshua Youngbuck. Joshua was a veteran of the Vietnam War where he earned the Medal of Honor for his bravery against a foreign enemy. Joshua used that same fortitude to battle within these very halls as a member of the United States Senate. Unfortunately, the battle against violence on our streets has claimed my precious Joshua. That's why I am here to ask you to pass the newly named Joshua Youngbuck Anti-Violence Act;" says Mrs. Youngbuck as members from both chambers rise to applaud.

Maryland Senator Phillip Leake understands the political chess move just perpetrated by Mrs. Youngbuck. There have been about 15 liberal Senators that have been on the fence. Senator Leake just heard the collective thud of some of those members falling to the other side.

# THE MARKET

It has been 10 days since the passage of the Prison Reform Act, the newly dubbed "Youngbuck Law." The passage of the Youngbuck Law has created a brand-new industry. Historically, crime prevention and the criminal justice system as a whole was never intended to make a profit. The thought was to reform wayward Americans away from their indiscretions while paying their debt to society. But the new law gave entrepreneurs a nudge toward making crime pay. The up-and-coming industry would allow states and the federal prison systems to contract the building of private prisons and to privatize its services. The criminals would stop being citizens that needed to be rehabilitated. Instead, they would be represented by a number that represents a cost on the private prisons bottom line. The 8MEN are celebrating their impending financial windfall at their Northwest Washington headquarters. It's hard to believe just two weeks ago the nation was in the grips of a fear of random violence on the cities' streets. But the 8MEN were happy because they laid the groundwork to take full advantage of the new landscape. The 8MEN have begun investing in companies that will be able profit from the increase of incarcerated Americans. The first industrial use of the incarcerated people will be purely as a workforce. Manufacturing companies like furniture makers, food processors and garment creators were going to be the first industries to take advantage of the cheap labor. The increasing power of the nation's employment unions has diminished the bottom line of many of the most profitable companies in American history. Fritz Kahn has partnered with some of those companies in an effort to regain their market share. The companies will pay the prisoners pennies on the dollar for essentially the same work done in their factories. The companies will pay the prisoners no more than five cents compared to the national minimum wage average of $2.65. Knowing that the companies would make a killing with his proposal, Kahn knew they would gladly pay his tax of 30 cents per prisoner per hour. Wesley Carter walks into the meeting room of the 8MEN with a look of disgust.

"What the hell did you do?" demands Carter.

"Mr. Carter you accuse me of so much. What are you referring to now?" asks Kahn.

"Youngbuck, you killed that young man. He didn't do anything wrong," declares Carter as the other 8MEN look at Kahn with puzzled looks.

"Didn't some Black drug addict kill him?" challenges a coy Kahn.

"This is some kind of joke to you?" questions a pissed Carter.

"Oh Mr. Carter, this is about money, and I never joke about that," utters Kahn.

"Everything is about money with you. That young man was what America is all about. And you killed him," asserts an infuriated Carter.

"You are right, he is everything America thinks it is. America over inflates its importance on the rest of the world without realizing it can be replaced," recites Kahn as he intensely looks at Carter.

# FINAL STRAW

Fritz Kahn knew that the murder of Senator Joshua Youngbuck would possibly be a bridge too far for Wesley Carter. Kahn knew that Wesley Carter looked at Youngbuck as a possible presidential candidate, but more importantly as an agent of change for the United States. Carter looked at Youngbuck as everything great about America and Kahn just snuffed him out. Kahn looked at the senator as a means to an end. In a way, Kahn wanted to stick his finger in Carter's eye giving him the reason to plot the ultimate demise of the 8MEN. Kahn has been pulling the strings of the group for several years, slowly destroying them from the inside out, but he knew at his core Wesley Carter was a true patriotic American. At some point, Carter would have to react. This act from Kahn may be the proverbial straw that breaks the camel's back. Carter has taken a diminished role within the 8MEN, but Kahn knew Carter would start to inquire what was going on. Kahn is beginning his final phase to destroy the 8MEN. He has called a meeting of his most trusted advisors in the states: Micquel Rojas and Wafai Rashad. The men met at an office space in New York.

"Glad you both were able to meet with me," says Kahn.

"Sure thing," says Wafai and Micquel.

"How is business?" asks Kahn of Rojas.

Rojas begins to laugh. He goes into his inside blazer pocket and pulls out an envelope.

"It has been well. We have orchestrated a silent hostile taken over of the Syndicate's business. The Italians being somewhat quiet has paid dividends. We have some problems with some of the Black gangs but in due time they will fall in line as well. So, I give you this with much pleasure," says Rojas as he slides the envelope to Kahn.

Kahn taps the envelope.

"Our agreed amount, correct?" asks Kahn.

Rojas nods his head in the affirmative.

"Great," says Kahn as he slides the envelope to Wafai.

"Mr. Rashad, I think it is time we get rid of the 8MEN. What do you think?" says Kahn.

Wafai Rashad replies with a devilish grin.

"Who do you want to start with?" asks Wafai.

"I don't know, surprise me," responds Kahn.

# TIME

Wesley Carter has finally reached his breaking point with Fritz Kahn. Carter has feared Kahn exposing him and the 8MEN's activities over the last quarter century. But the death of Michigan Senator Joshua Youngbuck was a bridge too far for Carter to stomach. He knows that Kahn will be coming for him. He knew he needed to prepare so he needs Danya and Teed to do some recon on Kahn. Carter meets Danya and Teed at Keleeha's soccer game at Ronald Watson Elementary in Upper Manhattan. Carter walks up to Teed. The game is in the second quarter when Carter arrives.

"How we doing?" asks Carter.

"Hey, we're scoreless right now. They just go up and down the field. And I can't get enough of it," says a dotting Teed.

Danya is cheering Keleeha a short distance away.

"I would have never pegged her for the domestic mommy type," says Carter about Danya's enthusiasm.

"Hey, children can do that to you," responds Teed. "I'm really happy for both of you. That little girl has seemed to have changed both of you," comments Carter.

"She has but that is not why you are here?" quips Teed.

"It's not. I'd love for you and Danya to do some recon on Kahn," says Carter.

"What are you looking for?" asks Teed.

Danya is about 20 yards away from the men. She can't hear their conversation, but she knows if Carter is involved it can't be good.

Teed and Carter walk away from the field to ensure some privacy.

"He means us no good. I want to figure what he is up to," says Carter.

"I always wondered why we didn't do this before now?" says Teed.

"I thought his motivation was wealth and power but there is something else there," Carter answers.

"What else could it be?" asks Teed.

"That's what I need you to find out. Go on, get back to the game," says Carter as he walks away from the field.

Moments later Danya walks up to Teed as he stands lost in thought.

"A penny for your thoughts," says Danya as she gives Teed a big bear hug.

"That's exactly what I needed," said Teed.

"What did Carter want?" asks Danya.

"Wanted us to do recon on Kahn," responds Teed.

"What happened?" Danya queries.

"Not sure, but it's got him spooked," answers Teed.

"You take care of that later, but right now let's get back to the game," Danya responds.

The couple hold hands on their way back to finish watching Keleeha's game.

# EVTVOLKERUNG

Fritz Kahn has begun to lay the groundwork for the last part of his diabolical plan to destroy America and the 8MEN. He has reached out to virologist Serge Schmidt. Schmidt is a former Nazi scientist. Schmidt came to the U.S. along with many other German scientists as a part of the secret Paperclip program. He is not a Nazi ideolog, and he is not a proponent of its Aryan Rhetoric, but he does believe that the world needs some type of depopulation occurrence. Schmidt is a part of the Evtvolkerung Society. The group advocates for the slowing of the world's population rates. It has championed methods like abortion, prophylactics, and oral contraception. But hardliners like Schmidt, believe the world needs more drastic action quickly. Fritz Kahn and Surge Schmidt have been acquainted for a number of years. The men are sharing a laugh in Kahn's New York office.

"The Americans are so clueless," says Schmidt as both men laugh.

"I may need you to consult on an idea of mine," says Kahn as he slides a file to Schmidt.

"I guess the fun times are over?" says Schmidt as he begins to flip through the pages of the file. "Anything look familiar?" asks Kahn.

Schmidt sits up straight. He is startled by what he is reading.

"Where did you get this?" asks Schmidt.

"From the U.S. Government. It was at its National Institutes of Health," says Kahn.

"Albrecht Krause created this. Brilliant man, but he was a bit of an asshole," says Schmidt.

"I've heard. Does it work?" asks Kahn.

"In theory, it does. The plan was to use this to euthanize the useless Jewish population and the gypsies after World War II using this method. Mon Fuhrer and his close circle grew tired at looking at the Jews and wanted them gone more quickly," says Schmidt with a hint of regret.

Kahn snaps Schmidt out of his thoughts.

"How would you institute this?" asks Kahn.

Schmidt begins to laugh.

"You can't do this now. Not here. In Germany, we were going to just line up the Jews and give them a shot. No one would have been the wiser. Because it is an autoimmune disease, it would affect each person differently. They would die at differing times but here, why would anyone line up for this willingly?" asks Schmidt.

"They line up because they think it is something else," responds Kahn.

"But why?" asks Schmidt.

"Come on. Your group has been looking for a reason to slow population. Here it is," says Kahn. "How do you pick who gets the shot?" curiously asks Schmidt.

"Start with the Negroes and the gays. Come up with a plan. If it works here, it can work all over the world," says Kahn.

Why would they voluntarily line up?" inquires a fiendish Schmidt.

# TIPPING POINT

Weeks have gone by since Fritz Kahn has tasked Surge Schmidt with coming up with a way to limit population growth. Dr. Schmidt has been trying to come up with a plan to quietly introduce Albrecht Krause's virus to the Black and homosexual communities. Schmidt has felt a bit conflicted; he is not a hater of the Black or homosexual communities, but he does believe that the world's population growth must be slowed. The last global population was estimated at a little over 4.3 billion people on January 1, 1978. According to the United Nations, it is estimated that the planet can sustain somewhere between 9 and 10 billion people. At the current rate, the world may reach its tipping point by 2040. In the past, Schmidt thought the Nazi philosophy of eliminating the handicapped and disabled could relieve some pressure on world population growth. At first, Schmidt was not a fan of Kahn's idea of limiting population growth. However, the idea has started to grow on him. Schmidt doesn't want to eliminate an entire subset of people, but he thinks if there is a precise target within the groups that could go a long way. He is watching the evening news at his Scarsdale, New York home. The news commentator is speaking about a prison riot. "Today's riot at the Rikers Island prison claimed the lives of 32 prisoners. It has been alleged that the fracas began over control of the New York City drug dealing territory between Black and Hispanic gangs," reports the commentator.

"Utterly ridiculous. None of them deserve to live," comments Schmidt to himself.

He then jumps to his feet. The nearly 75-year-old briskly walks to his home office. He begins to sketch out his plan on a chalk board in his office.

"Introduce the virus to large Black prison populations. Stay away from the more rural prison systems that may have a higher white population. Likely prisons: Rikers in New York and Folsom State in California. Say that the prisoners need to be vaccinated for flu or another airborne virus. It is important to keep the virus contained within the Black and gay communities. Make sure to inject all violent offenders. This just might work. If it works here, we can replicate all over the world. Get rid of all the undesirables," rambles Schmidt gleefully as he continues to write.

# PATIENT ZERO

Fritz Kahn's plan to introduce the virus into the general population needed an undetected entry point. That entry point was going to be Quinton Graham. Graham is a low-level drug dealer from 123rd Avenue in Harlem, New York. He was caught in a drug sting that netted the city over a million dollars. During the sting, Quinton Graham ran from the police. The police chased the young man into Central Park. They tackled him to ground and begin to savagely beat him.

"You fucking nigger," hollers a policeman as the group of police beat Graham. During the beating, he starts to cough up blood. A crowd starts to form. The police notice the crowd watching them and cease the beating. After pounding Graham to a pulp, the police handcuff him then sit him up. He has a bloodied face and has lost three teeth. "Officer requesting an ambulance for an injured offender," reports a policeman.

Hours later, Graham lays handcuffed to his hospital bed. His injuries are more apparent now, he is suffering from a broken jaw, nose and two ribs, lost four teeth and has a dislocated collar bone. Graham rests quietly in his bed. A masked hospital worker walks into the room. The worker walks over to Graham, making sure he is asleep. Once the masked person confirms the patient is asleep, a syringe pulled from the worker's pocket.

The shadowy figure injects Graham with an unknown substance. Afterward, the hooded man slinks out of the hospital room.

Several days later, Graham gets off a bus handcuffed, walking into the processing center at the New York City maximum correctional facility. He begins to cough as he enters the building. Days later the prison is filled with prisoners exhibiting flu-like symptoms, some are experiencing diarrhea and extreme dehydration. The facility's warden, Howard James, has tried to quarantine the sick from the healthy, but he is losing the battle. An official from the United States government reaches out to the warden to offer help. The warden agrees to the help. The officials showed up two days later. Government health officials set up an area to administer shots in the prison cafeteria. The healthy prisoners are lined up and given shots for the next four hours. Howard James walks to an area overlooking the cafeteria. The precision of the assembly line like distribution has pleased the warden.

"This place has been like an ER unit. I don't know how we thank you," conveys the warden.

"No need to thank me. We are here to eliminate the problem. In due time, all will be fine," implies Fritz Kahn.

# OMERTA

The Washington Sun is running a headline story "Assassination Conspiracy run by Shadow Government." The article tells a brief history of the Shadow Government's genesis. The group was fronted by the late South Carolina Senator, Hampton Capers. Capers conceived an elaborate cabal to evade many of the safeguards of the U.S. Constitution. He was running his scheme since the early 1940s. Understanding that he could not achieve his ultimate goals alone, Capers assembled a band of conspirators with a goal of "world domination." The cabal was made up of men from different walks of life. In polite society, these men would probably not cross paths, but the men came together to try to influence geopolitics while making a substantial profit. The alleged group is made up of an array of characters. Valerius Torrantio, reputed leader of the American Syndicate is alleged to be the muscle of the group. In exchange for safe passage of the syndicate's illicit activities, the syndicate provides the necessary arm twisting or breaking if necessary to accomplish the group's motives. The second member of the group was the late media mogul Murray Smith. Smith formerly known as Eithan Murray Smithburg came from Nazi Germany where he was a publisher. Smith used his position to run stories in favor of his group and promote the organization's propaganda. Hampton Capers helped Smith to obtain government backed financing and licensing at nearly no cost. From reports, it is believed that there are other members of the group, but Smith and Torrantio are believed to be major drivers of the group's mission.

Through his lawyer, Valerius Torrantio has been asked to come to the FBI's Midtown Manhattan office to answer some questions. Valerius and his attorney have been waiting for a little over an hour in an interrogation room.

"These folks don't give a shit about my time," recites Valerius as he looks at his expensive Rolex watch. "It's a tactic to make you nervous," theorizes the lawyer. "Nervous about what?" rebuts Valerius.

As if on cue, Assistant Director of the FBI Scott Davis enters the room.

"Gentlemen, my apologies for keeping you waiting," offers Davis.

"You drag my client down here then you have him waiting for over an hour?" asks the lawyer.

"Why am I here?" questions a testy Valerius.

"Mr. Torrantio, there have been some major allegations leveled against you. Have you read the paper?" inquires Davis.

"You requested my client to come here to answer for some fantastical story you read in the newspaper?" examines the lawyer.

"Today's meeting is just a conversation. If we aren't able to have a civil conversation where my questions are answered, then we may have to make things more formal," asserts a stern Davis.

"Are you threatening my client?" probes the lawyer. "No worries, ask your questions," utters Torrantio. "Great, did you know Hampton Capers and Murray Smith?" demands Davis.

Valerius has been questioned enough by the police over years to smell a trap. He is confident that they know he has had a relationship with these gentlemen.

"I did know them. I would run into them from time to time," admits Valerius.

"Did you have a business relationship with these men?" searches Davis.

Valerius looks intently at the Assistant Director.

"No, besides a good Cognac we don't have much in common," answers Valerius.

"So, drinking Cognac was the extent of your relationship with those men?" challenges Davis.

"Yup," responds Valerius.

"Well, Mr. Torrantio in that case, you are under arrest. We will have to make this more formal," affirms Davis.

# HEARINGS

The anonymity of the 8MEN was beginning to crash down around them. More specifically one of their charter members were being dragged into a national firestorm about the murdering of prominent Americans in the name of hefty profits. The explosive article about the assassinations of President John Fitzgerald Kennedy and Reverend Dr. Martin Luther King Jr. has touched a nerve in the nation. The recent Department of Justice interview of Valerius Torrantio has prompted more questions than answers raising the temperature of the issue. The United States Senate has decided to subpoena Mr. Torrantio for his testimony about the assassinations as well as to ask about some of the possible members of the shadowy group. The anticipation of Valerius' testimony has reached a fever pitch throughout the nation, so much so that the major news networks have decided to carry the hearing live. Valerius enters the Senate hearing room with a humble stroll through the crowd of photographers. Valerius has been getting advice from several attorneys to be forthcoming with his testimony but do not admit to anything. Valerius has been keeping his distance from his 8MEN brethren since the article publication because he knows that he is being stalked by the government and the pesky press. But he is extremely curious why the other surviving 8MEN were not mentioned in the newspaper article. Valerius walks to a long oak table that sits about 20 feet away from the group of 10 United States Senators.

"Good morning to my esteemed colleagues and to the American people watching at home. We have convened this hearing to investigate the murders of President Kennedy and Dr. Martin Luther King Jr. A recent article in the Washington Sun newspaper speaks to a cabal of Washington insiders and captains of industry conspiring to murder in the name of furthering their collective agendas."

Senator Robert Rivers hails from Modesto, California. He's been mentioned as an early favorite for the 1980 Republican Presidential nomination. Many Republican donors have expressed to Rivers' handlers that this hearing will be considered an audition for higher office. Rivers has promised to ham it up for the American people. "Our sole witness today is Mr. Valerius Torrantio. We will now swear in the witness. Mr. Torrantio please rise and raise your right hand and repeat after me," states Senator Rivers. "I Valerius Torrantio… (Valerius repeats). Swear that I will give truthful testimony so help me God… (Valerius repeats).

"Thank you, Mr. Torrantio," replies Senator Rivers.

"You are welcome," responds Valerius.

"Are you fully aware why you are here today?" inquires Senator Rivers.

Valerius leans over to ask his attorney a question.

"I am here because I have been accused of a crime," asserts Valerius.

"Mr. Torrantio, there have been reports that you have been in league with some gentlemen that have committed some major crimes," alleges Senator Rivers.

"Senator Rivers I am just as surprised by the article as well," retorts Valerius.

"Are you saying that you didn't know Senator Hampton Capers or Murray Smith?" doubts Senator Rivers.

"No, I knew both of them. But this story of shadow groups and all is a bit much," utters Valerius.

The senator points to some pictures.

"Let me point you to the pictures on our board. They show you with both Senator Capers and Mr. Murray Smith. Was this some type of meeting?" requests the Senator.

"Senator, I don't know what kind of answer I can give you. I knew these men but that is all," adds Valerius.

"What was the goal of your group? Was it to rule the world?" grills the Senator.

Valerius Torrantio is beginning to become irritated by the questions.

"I got nothing for you," answers a defiant Valerius.

"Mr. Torrantio, we want names of the other members of your group, and we want them now," demands Senator Rivers in a diminishing tone.

Valerius stands up and buttons his suit jacket and bellows, "I'M NOT GIVING YOU SHIT!"

A hush comes over the entire Senate chamber. The Senators on the panel look at each with horror. Valerius' attorney can do nothing but put his head in his hands because of the embarrassment.

Valerius sits down.

"I guess I fucked up," discloses Valerius under his breath.

"Sergeant at Arms, take Mr. Torrantio into custody. This hearing is adjourned," states Senator Rivers.

# BOOGIE DOWN

There is no illegal drug market like the urban jungle of New York City. The city has always had an intimate relationship with illicit drugs dating back to the turn of the century. Drugs have always been a part of America's fabric, those who sold them did not advertise and those that purchased them were discreet. Oddly enough, the American Mafia have kept the drug trade out of the spotlight. The Mafia has gone to great lengths to keep drugs out of so-called good neighborhoods and away from the business districts. Recently, the heads of the five Italian Mafia families were indicted on Racketeering Influence Corrupt and Organizations Act (RICO) charges. Along with the Senate Hearings on assassinations involving Valerius Torrantio, the Mafia has been forced to pull back from its normal public posture. Unlike other U.S. cities, New York's drug trade is divided equally among the Mafia families to avoid any unwanted territorial disputes. With the Mafia is retracting its public persona, it has left a power vacuum in the city that the up-and-coming dealers have tried to fill. The once defined boundaries have been crossed, causing an uptick in high-profile murders and an increase in police activity trying to thwart the resurgence. Knowing that New York City's drug hierarchy was different from all the other cities he had encountered, Micquel Rojas decided to take another approach. Rojas has gathered some of the big players at a vacant storefront in the North Bronx. Lonnie "The Glove" Williams, a former basketball playground legend from Harlem shot up the ranks after the demise of former Harlem chiefs Nicky Barnes and Frank Lucas. Luis Grillo is a Cuban immigrant who has stepped up his efforts to claim the South Bronx. Andel Garnett has been making a major play for parts of Queens and Brooklyn in the Mafia's absence. All three men are flanked by several men from their crews. There is a noticeable tension between Lonnie Williams and Luis Grillo. The men's organizations have been exchanging gunfire and dead bodies over the last six months. The battle has claimed the life of Williams' brother Armond and Grillo's cousin Ricardo.

"Gentlemen I am truly thankful you have chosen to meet today," mentions Rojas.

"Why are we here?" asks an impatient Garnett.

"I asked to meet with you to propose a partnership," responds Rojas.

"Are you fucking kidding me?" asserts Williams.

"I would never partner with this la mierda," admits an angry Grillo in Williams' direction.

Several of Rojas' men have to separate Williams and Grillo.

"Gentlemen, emotions are obviously running high. I want to triple your profits, but in order to do that I need all three of you to partner with us," discloses Rojas.

"Why do all three of us have to partner up?" questions Garnett.

"Because as partners we leverage the product which allows us to form an alliance against those who will challenge us," advises Rojas.

"Not that I want this deal, but what happens when the Italians come back looking for their territory?" pushes back Williams.

"We would fight them. We would have our army to withstand them. The Mafia is strong because they are organized. Let's organize," offers a sensible Rojas. "How do I know Mr. Williams and his people won't come for me or my people?" inquires Grillo. Rojas walks over to Lonnie Williams and looks him in his eyes, "Cause if Mr. Williams breaks the agreement, I will cut his heart out," claims Rojas as he turns toward Grillo.

"Anybody that breaks this deal dies. Am I clear?" asks Rojas as he looks into Grillo's eyes. "Understood," responds a slightly frightened Grillo.

# THE GODFATHER

Don Tommaso Torrantio has not touched foot on American soil since he semi-retired back in 1940. Don Torrantio turned over control of the global syndicate to his son Valerius. The Torrantio family has controlled much of the illicit vices of prostitution and drugs in Central Europe and Northern Africa for several centuries. But the bulk of the money the syndicate that the Torrantio family has controlled was also very instrumental in financing businesses. Developing and maintaining real estate has proven to be just as lucrative as their foray into the illicit vices. Because of their successes, the Torrantio Syndicate was approached by the Lumiere to partner in the effort to dominate the civilized world. Up to now, the partnership has been running like a well-oiled machine. Don Torrantio was paid a visit to his home in Milan by Fritz Kahn. The two men have not seen each other in over five years, so the retired Godfather was quite concerned for the impromptu meeting. The two men have always shared a respectful relationship but knew that the other was capable of treacherous deeds. The somewhat frail Don entertains Fritz Kahn in his art room. Kahn is amazed by two of the paintings hanging from the walls.

"Each time I come here; I am even more amazed by these two paintings," remarks an awestruck Kahn. "Those are two of my most prized possessions. Alfredo and Paulino Verde captured two distinct moments in American history," replies Don Torrantio.

Alfredo Verde's portrait depicts Christopher Columbus descending from the Mayflower and Paulino's painting illustrates hundreds of Negro soldiers marching toward the U.S. Capitol after the Civil War.

"Both are very powerful pieces of art. But I am sure you didn't come here for that," concedes a leery Don Torrantio.

"Can't get anything past you," admits Kahn.

"My body is fleeting, not my mind," says Don Torrantio.

"That being said. You are aware of your son's activities with the group of 8MEN?" asks Kahn.

"I am," responds Don Torrantio.

"His group was responsible for the death of a family member of mine. I cannot let that pass Don Torrantio," says Kahn.

"Have you come here to ask me to sanction the murder of my son? Is this why my son is in an American prison?" asks an angry Don Torrantio.

"I am not here to sanction your son's death, but he needs to pay for his part in the murder," responds a measured Kahn.

Kahn knows that the Torrantio Family carries major weight within the Lumiere, and he would rather not tangle with Don Torrantio.

"Since you helped put my son in that prison, how does my son get out of prison?" asks Don Torrantio.

"Your son will be given the choice to self-deport. He needs to take the choice," suggests Kahn.

Don Torrantio is very bothered by the choice that he is being given.

"You should have informed me before now," adds an irate Don Torrantio.

"My apologies for not informing you," says a softened Kahn.

"Mr. Kahn, I don't like this at all. But what's done is done. My son will receive safe passage back to Italy, correct?" challenges a calculating Don Torrantio.

"Yes," Kahn answers.

"Then I agree. But rest assured that if anything happens to my son. I will come out of retirement and destroy everything," proclaims a deliberate Don Torrantio.

# PAPI

After his disastrous Senate testimony, Valerius Torrantio was taken back to the Ossining Correctional Facility (known as Sing Sing) in Westchester County, New York to await formal charges. Officially, Valerius Torrantio has not been charged with any offenses, but there have been whispers of the RICO act and some obscure treasonous laws from the early 1800s. Making Valerius even more nervous is the absence of Wesley Carter. He understands that Carter should keep his distance, but Carter not reassuring him in some kind of way has the Mafia chief a bit anxious. Valerius has been confined to a separate wing of the prison only locked away with his thoughts. The conspiratorial thoughts have begun to creep in. He has played out the possibility that he will be the fall guy of some the greatest crimes in U.S. history. His thoughts were that the Senate was setting him up to be the surviving member of a treasonous circle. Valerius is awakened from a mid-afternoon nap in his cell. The prison guard walks a visibly confused Valerius to an old multi-purpose room. There waiting for Valerius is a frail Don Tommaso Torrantio. Valerius rubs his eyes in disbelief of the vision in front of him.

"This must be a dream. This can't be," says a joyful Valerius Torrantio.

"No, my son, it is me," answers a weak Don Torrantio.

In this moment, Valerius is overcome with relief. Valerius runs to give his father a hug.

"I am so glad you are here," conveys Valerius.

"How are you holding up?" asks Don. Torrantio. "I've been better," affirms Valerius as he chuckles. "Valley, this situation is serious," mentions Don Torrantio.

"I kinda figured..." Valerius is interrupted.

"Your group killed the cousin of the leader of the Lumiere," discloses Don Torrantio.

"Who is the leader, who is his cousin?" requests Valerius.

"Fritz Kahn, his cousin was J. Edgar Hoover," declares Don Torrantio.

"WHAT THE FUCK? No fucking way! He has basically been running our group over the past five years," admits an exasperated Valerius.

"He has been lying in wait for his opportunity to get you all," suggests Don Torrantio.

"To get us?" quires Valerius.

"He has been plotting to kill all of you since entrance to your group," claims Don Torrantio.

"So why did he tell you?" questions Valerius.

"He needed to get you out of the way. You provide the muscle. Once you are out of the way, the 8MEN don't have protection. And the Torrantio family is a part of the Lumiere," divulges a regretful Don Torrantio.

"Papi, you knew who this man was, and you never said anything," says a disappointed Valerius.

"I never thought he was up to anything like this," affirms Don Torrantio.

"So, you knew he wanted to kill me," pushes back Valerius.

"No… no. he knows he could never touch you. That's why you are here. He wanted to force you out of the country. You knowing you could get the death penalty could make you leave the country. And I am here to make sure you come home.

Please son," pleads a passionate Don Torrantio.

# FATHER'S SINS

Throughout history men have thought to impose their world view on the wider society. Adolf Hitler believed the Jewish people were the bane of Western Europe, and the only cure for Western Europe was their extermination. Hitler's mindset was not borne of Germany, it was given birth by Louis Assassiz. Assassiz was a Harvard professor that taught Polygenism. The discredited study theorized that all the differing races were different species. The study categorized the races from top to bottom with white people at the top of the species hierarchy, thus giving false validation for white supremacy. It is that line of thinking that has put Fritz Kahn on a course to limit the number of people on the planet. Kahn figured to be as consequential as the aforementioned historical figures, but his intention was not necessarily a world view, he wants to limit population by limiting who gets to live. The Gefangis company has completed its work on the Autoimmune Virus. The virus would affect people unwittingly through exchange of body fluids. The virus will be introduced to the Black, Hispanic and homosexual populations. Kahn has been eager to get the virus out to the wider population, but he wanted to ensure that he had a backup plan in case things went sideways. Fritz Kahn is meeting with Maximilian Love at a small off the books warehouse in Yonkers, New York. The men meet a little after 8 pm. The facility has played host to many of the Gefangis organization's top secret biological projects. Love has welcomed Kahn's project with open arms. With Kahn injecting nearly $200 million into the company coffers, Love has made sure to keep Kahn happy. The men are walking through the warehouse.

"This is impressive. How long have you had this facility?" asks an inquisitive Kahn.

Love responds proudly," This facility has housed many of the viruses we created under the Reich. Much of the research was not completed by the end of the war. The U.S. opened up all its resources to us. We have brought many biological weapons to fruition."

Kahn has a moment of clarity. He remembers that his twin brothers were experimented on under the Nazis. Kahn is angered but controls his feelings to hurt Love.

"We have perfected many viruses. They are now ready to be put into the world. Starting with your virus," suggests Love as he points an obscure container. Kahn walks over to container.

"So, this is it?" inquires Kahn.

"It is," answers Love.

"Thank you for your hard work. The mission is now going to be completed," declares Kahn as he pulls a .45 revolver and shoots Maximilian Love twice in the heart.

Love is in shock and stumbles into a cabinet.

"Why? I did everything you asked," stammers Love. "And I thank you, but men like you killed my family," replies Kahn as he shoots Love in the head.

# THE SCORE

Richard Teed is staking out Fritz Kahn's modest New Rochelle home. He has been watching Kahn's comings and goings over the last week. On this early Sunday afternoon, Teed is joined by The Squirrel. Teed has observed Kahn leaving his house pretty much every day at 9:30 am, weekends included. It is an understatement to say the man is consistent about his time. Teed and The Squirrel watch from a safe distance as the predictable Kahn leaves his house.

"Wow, right on time, you weren't bullshitting," admits The Squirrel.

"He leaves the house and goes to the city. And he's there for the duration of the day," claims Teed.

"Have you seen anyone else there?" asks The Squirrel.

"Not really, there's a housekeeper that comes on Wednesday and Saturday around noon," mentions Teed. The Squirrel asks, "any idea what you are looking for?"

"Not sure, Carter is feeling really uneasy about this guy."

The Squirrel says, "I haven't always liked him, but Carter's instincts are normally pretty spot on."

Teed adds, "I'm guessing Carter wants something to leverage against Kahn."

The Squirrel retorts, "Makes sense, so you want me to stay?"

"I should be alright. I thought you had something in the Bronx," implies Teed.

"Shit, I do. I have a meeting with the Rojas people. Something about those folks doesn't sit right with me," The Squirrel said.

"Seems like a lot of that going around," said Teed.

The men share a laugh as Teed exits the car. Teed walks to the rear of the house and notices an opened window. He looks in the window. Not seeing anyone, he pops out the screen and enters the room. After gaining access, Teed walks through the house very carefully looking for an office. He finds the office and marvels how clean and orderly the office and the house are. Teed sits at Kahn's desk trying to figure out the next move. He decides to tug on the desk drawers. All of them are secured. Teed finds a letter opener on the top of the desk. He begins to haphazardly pry at each drawer. The first two drawers bare no fruit, but the third drawer shows some promise. There are several files but Teed sees one labeled, "8MEN."

"What the hell?" Teed asks himself. He realizes the files he has stumbled across are the same files he and Danya read after J. Edgar Hoover's death. "Why does he have these?" a puzzled Teed asks himself. Teed continues to root through the files. He is startled when he sees a list that is labeled, "My Vengeance." The names read: Murray Smith, Cecil Thomas, Maximilian Love, Wesley Carter, Danya Franck, The Squirrel, and Richard Teed.

"Shit, I gotta get out of here," Teed says to himself.

He neatly puts everything back. Teed has to get to Danya. He is rushing toward the front door. Out of nowhere Teed is hit in the back of head, knocking him unconscious. He falls violently to the floor.

# THE BRONX

New York City has been caught in a lot of upheaval over the last three years. The city had a major police corruption scandal, were gripped by the Son of Sam murders and the looming possibility of the city falling into financial ruin by declaring its first bankruptcy. All these issues played into a depressed city that felt no reason to hope for a brighter day. The Rojas organization has taken full advantage of the city's hopelessness. While businesses of all stripes are failing at record rates in New York City, the Rojas organization's market share of the illegal drug trade has grown exponentially. The organization has diversified its investment in the New York City drug trade. Rojas doesn't just make money from hand-to-hand sales on the street, they are also making money from wholesale transactions to competing dealers. The Rojas organization was careful to partner with the Italians in certain areas to avoid any potential turf wars while co-oping their knowledge and muscle. Micquel Rojas could have never dreamed that he would take over the New York City drug trade without any turf wars and any major causalities of his crew. Every enclave of the city that is populated by Black and brown people are feeling the success of the Rojas organization's fortune through the pain of increased drug addiction and increased joblessness from the hollowed-out communities. Rojas called a meeting of all the partnering organizations.

He believed in sharing the spoils of his success. The experiment of bringing warring factions together in the name of financial power has been a success. Rojas has set a meeting in an abandoned warehouse in the North Bronx for the top brass of those running drugs in New York City. Micquel Rojas arrives at the warehouse with all in attendance. Following Rojas into the meeting are three men carrying two large duffle bags each. The men place two bags at the feet of each organization head.

"Gentlemen, I have a gift for you. You should share with your men," suggests a joyful Rojas as the men look into the bags.

The men are excited to see the money.

"So, what's this for?" asks Lonnie Williams.

"We have a great partnership and we have taken over this city. Just wanted to share," adds Rojas as several gentlemen dressed as waiters come into the room wheeling tables of food and drinks. "Gentlemen, enjoy yourselves," offers Rojas as he exits the room.

Moments later a barrage of gunfire erupts. The perfectly planned attack takes the gangsters by surprise. All but Lonnie Williams are immediately hit by bullets. Lonnie is able to shoot five members of the Rojas gang. As he makes a run for the front door, he is shot in the back and in the leg. An injured Lonnie stumbles out of the warehouse and staggers to a nearby alley. As he lay bleeding, The Squirrel pulls up.

"God damn Glove!" exclaims a surprised Squirrel.

"What happened?"

A gasping Williams utters, "Motherfucking Rojas double crossed us."

"Never trusted him," admits The Squirrel as he tries to stop Williams from bleeding.

The life begins to drain from Williams.

"Stay with me," pleads The Squirrel as he is now drenched in Williams' blood. Williams' body goes limp.

"Damn," says The Squirrel.

# COUP

On the other side of the world, Wafai Rashad and Cecil Thomas have traveled to the outskirts Abadan, Iran. The pair have traveled to the Middle East to deliver munitions to student revolutionaries. To this point, the students have been peacefully protesting their disputes with Shah Mohammad Reza Pahlavi's government for the better part of two years now. Until recently, the country had been marred in financial straits with mounting inflation and the overwhelming distrust of the Shah's westernized government. The Iranian people are leery of anything with western roots. It is widely believed that the Americans and the Brits helped the Iranian military overthrow Premier Mohammad Mosaddeq's government. This move paved the way for the western-backed Shah Pahlavi's ascension. After Pahlavi's ascent, western companies began to profit off the Iranian natural resources. Many from the land formerly known as Persia, hold the governments of the U.S. and Great Britain responsible for fleecing their country. Wealthy American and British companies have gobbled up the land rights to oil deposits without giving much back to the country. The country of Iran has profited greatly off of the world's consumption of oil, but that wealth has not been spread to the people equally. The Shah has tried to bring the Islamic Republic toward a more western way of life. He has gotten rid of many Islamic norms such as women having to wear hijabs and being relegated to second class citizenship. Until recently, university students have been protesting The Shah and his oppressive government. Even though many of the heavily female led protesters appreciated many of the relaxed measures toward women, they still believed that Islam should be central to Iranian life.

A little over a week ago, dozens of protesters gathered in Tehran at the busy hub in Jalen Square to continue their protest of the government. The day before the protest, the Shah had declared martial law. It was thought that the protesters were thumbing their noses at the Shah and the government. The spirited demonstration descended into a confrontation between the students and the agitated military. It is unknown the exact events, but the army surrounded the protestors and began to shoot haphazardly. In that moment, the protest took on a life of its own. No longer were the students merely speaking about the Iranian government cozying up to the west, now the students knew that the Shah had to go for them to simply survive. Since the tragedy in Jalen Square, the students have been building coalitions with unaligned partners. Previously, the protestors would have never thought to ally with the cleric class but with the Shah's crack down on civil discord has made the students and the clerics strange bedfellows.

Wafai Rashad and Cecil Thomas are driving a white box truck on their way to meet the students.

The two men have barely spoken since leaving a small airstrip outside of Tehran.

"So, students want to take on the government huh?" says Cecil Thomas as they continue down a bumpy dusty road.

"The young people want their freedom. It is not falsely promised to everyone like it is in America," snaps Wafai.

Cecil Thomas is visibly taken aback by Wafai's comment.

"You think people in America aren't free?" questions Thomas.

"There are some who are free, but many aren't," implies Wafai.

"You aren't from America. How would you know?" quires Thomas. "That's just it because I am not from America, so I don't have to participate in the ruse. Your country was created solely for the purpose of exploiting a foreign land for natural resources and its people," theorizes Wafai.

"What ruse? Christopher Columbus discovered America," alleges Cecil Thomas.

The always serious Wafai Rashad breaks into extreme laughter as the men pull up to a farmhouse where five people are waiting. Thomas and Rashad descend from the truck, Wafai is still laughing to himself. As the men walk toward the farmhouse, the students meet them. "You are Wafai Rashad?" asks Yasmin Tousi. Yasmin Tousi is the student leader of many of the protests and public appearances of the last two years. She and her group of protesters have been a modest group asking for a sit-down discussion to help solve some of the public discord. But the tragedy at Jalen Square has changed everything. Tousi has passionately spoken at rallies since the murders. Much of the Iranian public have ignored the students gripes until now. There is a brewing discontent that is starting to catch on with the average person. The discussion has gone from finding middle ground that everyone can agree to and now the protesters want nothing less than the Shah resigning. The students know that they have turned up the rhetoric against the Shah and they know they must be prepared for a confrontation with the army.

"I am. Assalamu alaikum," responds Wafai. "Wa alaikum salaam," says Tousi. "This is Cecil Thomas," responds Wafai. Tousi responds, "Greetings, Mr. Thomas. Mr. Rashad, do you speak Farsi? My English is very rough." Wafai says, "I do," as he turns to Thomas. "I will speak with her in Farsi and let you know the verdict," advises Wafai. He begins to speak. The guns are in the back of the truck. They walk to the back of the truck where Tousi's associates take the guns out. The men start to examine the guns and the other munitions including grenades and rocket launchers. They are impressed with the merchandise.

Tousi says in Farsi, "my associates are impressed." Wafai answers, "I'm glad. So, we have deal?"

Tousi answers, "We do."

"Allah be with you," humbly says Wafai.

"He is. Our mission is a righteous one," affirms Tousi. Wafai is impressed by the student's resolve.

"We have a deal," declares Wafai to Cecil Thomas. "Great," adds Thomas.

# ASIATIC CHEETAH

The Arabian Peninsula is home to one of the most dynamic animals in Asia, the Asiatic cheetah. The Asiatic cheetah has evolved into an apex predator in the region. Unlike its African cousin, the Asiatic cheetah stands atop of the ecosystem in the region. Not scientifically proven, but it is believed that the big cat is larger than its relative because of its lack of competition for food. The Asiatic cheetah has attracted the attention of poachers and hunters wanting to take the big cat down. After taking care of their big gun sale with the student revolutionaries, Wafai Rashad decided to stop off at a hunting reserve to get in some hunting before heading back to the states. Wafai traveled as a child to the reserve with his father to hunt big game. In the short time since his childhood, the once vibrant species has become endangered. Because of the endangered status, hunting the big animal has become more exclusive as well as expensive. During his time in the Air Force, Cecil Thomas rarely shot his side arm. He was a great pilot but always expressed that he felt ashamed that he did not participate in hand-to-hand combat like most soldiers in World War II. He believes hunting quenches that blood thirst. Wafai and Thomas have been hunting for hours. They have run across several small animals during their hunt. So far, they have bagged a wild pig, a couple of foxes and a few hares. But the reason for the trip has evaded the pair. The men sit in a well camouflaged hunter's perch.

"We have done well," offers Wafai as he looks at the carcasses of their kills.

"We have, but we have to get a cheetah," says an excited Cecil Thomas.

"Never thought of you as a blood thirsty person," mentions Wafai.

"Not blood thirsty, I enjoy the hunt. Puts me in touch with my macho side," insists Thomas.

"Interesting," scoffs Wafai as he gives Thomas a condensing look.

"What does that mean?" asks Thomas.

"You are a big war hero; I just thought you would have many stories of face-to-face combat," implies Wafai.

He knows Thomas was a pilot and had no opportunity to fight face to face. He used this opportunity to insult Thomas.

"No, I was a pilot," reminds Thomas.

"Hey, you turned the tide from the air, right?" asserts Wafai as he spots a small group of gazelles in the distance.

"You may just get your prize. You see those gazelles on the horizon? We are getting close to dusk. If there are any cheetahs in the area, they will come," claims Wafai.

Hesitantly Thomas asks, "So what do we do?"

"Take this rifle and go to that tree over there.

Wafai points to a tree about 50 yards from the hunter's perch.

"This is your big catch. You will hang it in your office," adds Wafai.

Wafai goads the hesitant Thomas out of the perch. Thomas stands vigilant at the tree for several minutes when out of nowhere a lone cheetah appears about 300 yards away. The cheetah is stalking the unsuspecting gazelles as it is being stalked by Thomas. Realistically, the cheetah is in range for a good shot, but Thomas doesn't have a great deal of confidence in the shot. He continues to track the feline. He wants to wait until he hits 250 yards away to get the perfect shot. Thomas must be careful; the Asiatic cheetah is known to be very aggressive toward humans and have been known to them. Thomas tracks the cat for another 30 yards through the scope. He is sweating profusely. It is an unbelievably hot day, but the intensity of the moment has overwhelmed him to point he has to wipe sweat from his eyes. Thomas' hands begin to tremble as the cheetah enters the point of no return. Thomas musters up the courage and lets off the first shot. The shot strikes the animal. While the shot is on target, it is not fatal. Thomas checks the gun, realizing he has another bullet. The cheetah notices where the shot came from and zeroes in on Thomas standing a good 200 yards away. The cat abandons the kill of the gazelles in favor of going after Thomas. Thomas sees that the Cheetah is coming for him, he readies his gun for another shot. The cheetah has begun his sprint toward Thomas. As the cat reaches 100 yards from its prey, Thomas lets off another shot, seeming to hit the cheetah but still not taking it down. Thomas realizes he will not be able to subdue the cheetah with his gun. The 60-plus year-old Thomas begins a light sprint toward the hunter perch.

"Wafai, help me!" desperately says an out of breath Thomas.

Wafai takes out a cigar and cuts it and begins to slowly light the cigar.

Thomas is about 10 yards from the tree. He seems like he is going to evade the cheetah. Wafai kicks away the ladder leading to the hunter's perch. The cheetah is closing fast.

"Why would you?" demands Thomas as the cheetah jumps on his back.

Thomas tries to fight back against the cheetah but the cat slices off several fingers from Thomas' left hand. Causing Thomas enormous pain. Wafai watches from the perch savoring the moment another member of the 8MEN will perish. The pain of his lost digits will pale in comparison to the death blow that the circling cheetah is about to deliver to Cecil Thomas. In seconds Thomas is dead as the animal begins to maul him. Wafai Rashad salutes the Cheetah on his kill.

# SING SING

It has been two weeks since Wesley Carter watched the Senate Hearings debacle. He watched the proceedings knowing the 8MEN were now over for sure. Carter was concerned for his friend and quite frankly worried about when someone would be coming to knock on his door. Because of the spotlight placed on Torrantio, Carter waited for an opportune time to slip into the Sing Sing facility to gauge what exactly was going on with Torrantio. Valerius Torrantio decided to take the deal to leave the U.S. He is due to leave the Ossining facility later today and boarding a flight destined for Palermo, Italy. He is packing up a few knick knacks in preparation for his departure.

"Psst." A prison guard motions to Valerius.

The cell door opens and the guard walks Valerius to the same multipurpose room he visited with his father just a week before. Waiting for Valerius this time in the covert space was Wesley Carter.

"You look well," remarks a guarded Carter.

"I'm making it," responds Valerius.

Carter walks over to Valerius and begins to pat him down. The government has been known to bug prisoners when they believe they will meet a high value target. Carter is concerned for his friend, but he was not going to take any chances.

"What the hell?"

Valerius is interrupted as Carter pulls out a device to sweep for any electronic recording devices. Carter feels at ease since his sweep didn't come up with anything.

"Are you fucking kidding me? You think I'm a rat?" declares a pissed Torrantio.

Carter walks over to give him a hug.

"Really? You lost your mind on national TV. I know they have offered you all kinds of deals to bring down the rest of the 8MEN," rebuts Carter.

"Actually, they didn't. This whole thing is fucked up. It has all been Kahn. He has been behind everything. He killed Love, Bowen and we were last on his list," affirms Torrantio.

"What?" challenges a bewildered Carter.

"This whole thing was about revenge," states Torrantio.

"Revenge, we never did anything to him," answers Carter.

"Yeah, we did. We killed his cousin," admits Torrantio.

"His cousin, who was his cousin?" questions Carter.

"Hoover was his cousin. GOD DAMN J. EDGAR HOOVER!" emphatically says Torrantio.

The news hits Carter like a ton of bricks.

"And this fucker is no regular guy. He runs the Lumiere," adds an agitated Torrantio.

"What is the Lumiere," inquires Carter.

"You've heard of the Illuminati?" asks Torrantio.

"Of course," implies Carter as he is trying to grasp what is going on.

"The Illuminati is a ghost tale. The Lumiere is the real shit. They have their hand in everything in Europe, Northern Africa and parts of Asia. Finance, real estate, oil, you name it. America was untapped. Hoover was going to bring us closer to them. But once we killed Hoover, Kahn was pissed and decided to make us pay slowly. But his intent was to kill us all," divulges Torrantio.

"How did you find this out?" quizzes Carter.

"My father, my family is a part of the Lumiere," discloses a dejected Torrantio.

"So now what?" asks Carter.

"He is cleaning house. He is killing everyone but me," alleges Torrantio.

"Why not you?" asks an inquisitive Carter.

"He can't afford to go to war with my family. He went through all of this to get me out of the way. Now he will be coming for you," states Torrantio.

"He won't have to come. I will find him," replies a determined Carter.

# MEMORY LANE

The revelation of Kahn's identity has sent former Director Carter into a rage. He feels his intelligence has been insulted and him personally being out thought. There were very few times in his life that Carter didn't think he was the smartest guy in the room. Kahn had taken over Carter's clandestine group without as much as a struggle because Carter thought he would otherwise be blackmailed. All the while Kahn was plotting to kill Carter and his cohorts anyway. Carter speeds down Interstate 95 from Sing Sing to confront Kahn at his mid-town Manhattan office. There are a bevy of thoughts going through his mind. He thinks about how Kahn had set him up. Inviting him to the conference in France, feeling him out, making him a mark. Thinking about the ruse makes Carter angry and ashamed that he didn't see it coming all along.

"He fucking played me. Fuck!" admits Carter to himself as he smacks the steering wheel with disgust.

Carter thought to himself, he was supposed be one of the savviest intelligence agents in the world, he created the CIA for Pete's sake! How did he not make the connection?

"Why didn't I run background on Kahn? It would've shown his and Hoover's relationship. I thought his deception was based on the quest for power, not for revenge. Fuck!" exclaims Carter to himself as he finally realizes the totality of the situation.

He continues to think back over the years since Kahn's hostile takeover of the 8MEN.

"I let him kill Murray right in front of my face and I didn't do a god damn thing about it. I let my best friend die without lifting a finger. I lied to his son because I am coward," declares Carter to himself as he begins to weep.

He is overcome with emotion. He pulls off the interstate near White Plains and begins to sob.

"God, I didn't want any of this to happen. I wanted America to be the greatest county in world history and I wanted to make some money to boot. But not all this death, not the destabilization of the country. I sat by and watched him slowly destroy this country and kill my friends. I didn't want this," claims Carter as he reaches into his glove compartment.

Carter pulls out his .38 revolver. He looks at his gun fondly.

"I have tried to never use a gun myself. But this death, Kahn's death, I must carry out myself," says a determined Carter as if the .38 revolver were a person.

Over the years if Carter needed someone killed, he contracted someone to take care of it. He always kept his hands clean.

"God, I am sorry for all that I have done. This is my mess. I need to clean this up today," recites a resolute Carter.

He wipes the tears from his face and gets back on the interstate speeding toward Manhattan.

An hour later Carter arrives in Midtown. He pulls in front of the building at 3243 Washington Street. He remembers the building has a large security presence in the lobby. Carter wants to avoid any confrontation that may slow him down. He decides to go into the building's underground garage. Since it is after 5 pm, Carter should get a space, and he is banking on the security being more relaxed. Carter parks a short distance from the elevator. Before getting out of the car he safely places the .38 revolver in his waistband.

"Here we go," affirms a decisive Carter as he walks toward the garage elevator.

# SUNSET

The elevator door to Kahn's office opens with a determined Carter standing in the doorway. Kahn is on the phone when he sees an unamused Carter starring back at him. Carter pulls his gun from waistband.

"Let me call you back," says Kahn to the person on the phone.

Carter checks the safety on his gun.

"Mr. Carter, you finally found the balls I didn't think you had," insults Kahn.

Quietly Carter steps toward Kahn as he continues to stare.

"I'm guessing you had a conversation with Mr. Torrantio. And he clued you into who I really am. You were thought to be the savviest intelligence officer in the world," scoffs Kahn.

"This ends today," barks Carter at Kahn.

Kahn starts to laugh uncontrollably.

"It will undoubtedly end today. You are the last of the 8MEN. I guess this is somewhat poetic.

The call I was just on, confirmed the death of Cecil Thomas," discloses Kahn.

"Cecil is in Iran," responds Carter.

Kahn responds, "He was eaten by a pretty pissed cheetah. Seems Thomas was not a good marksman. And late last night I killed Baron Richter with this gun."

Carter has a look of confusion on his face. Kahn continues, "My apologies, you probably didn't know that was the original name of Maximilian Love or whatever he was calling himself. He was a Nazi that you gave cover to," states Kahn in a sadistic tone.

"You are right. I didn't know who you are but none of that matters now," utters Carter.

"I'm so glad we can talk freely. I thought the great Wesley Carter would have figured all this out years ago. At first, I simply wanted to kill you and the 8MEN, but then I wanted to destroy the very thing you held dear, your beloved America. Most of you couldn't agree on anything but the ideals of this God forsaken place. You know when we threw Murray Smith from the train, I always wished that you would have been the one to confront me. It would have been so sweet to have seen you ripped apart by those rocks.

But killing Senator Youngbuck was a great consolation. You thought he would be America's great hope. I want to see America burn," declares an infuriated Kahn.

"You want to destroy America because I killed your demented cousin. Since we are being truthful and all. I had a certain joy watching the life drain from Edgar. I wish I could do it again and again and again," taunts Carter with a smile on his face. Kahn screams in anger as he pulls his gun.

"I'm gonna kill you," affirms Kahn as he jumps up from his desk pointing his gun at Carter. Carter shoots at Kahn, he misses. Kahn returns fire and hits Carter in the leg. Carter stumbles in pain. Carter shoots hitting Kahn in the shoulder. Kahn shoots back hitting Carter once in the chest forcing him to drop the gun. Both men are spent and feeling their injuries, but Carter is more seriously injured. Kahn checks for injuries, realizing it is just his shoulder, gets up. He looks over to see Carter laying on his back bleeding from his chest. Kahn stumbles over to Carter.

"So, it looks like the best man is going win," alleges Kahn as he fumbles to fill his .38 with bullets. Carter is slowly drowning in his own blood as he attempts to speak.

"Teed will kill you," recites a choking Carter.

"Those are your last words. Rest assured, Teed and Franck are next. Take that thought to the afterlife," says Kahn as he shoots Carter in head.

# THE DOCTOR

The Squirrel speeds down White Plains Road in the Bronx heading south with a bloodied Lonnie Williams clinging to life in his passenger seat. The Squirrel's mind is going a mile a minute. He knows he must get his childhood friend to a doctor, but he also knows that a shooting victim attracts unwanted questions and will cost him precious time that he doesn't have. In his line of business, The Squirrel sometimes encounters some violence, and he needs to have someone on standby to help his street soldiers heal without being bombarded with any pesky questions about a shootout. Harvey met The Squirrel in Korea when he saved a private from his platoon who was badly injured and left for dead. The private was on a scout team that was investigating the progress of Korean forces from the North. There was a small gun fight where the private was shot in the neck. Without Harvey's quick response the private would have died. Ever since then, The Squirrel has sworn by Harvey's lifesaving skills. In another life Troy Harvey would have been a world-renowned surgeon, but in this life, he was a former Army field medical technician who served in World War II and the Korean War. Harvey garnered a reputation for saving the lives of soldiers that others couldn't save. He specialized in delicately removing shrapnel from the bodies of injured soldiers. A skill he learned while a student at Howard University's medical school. After the Korean War, a broken Harvey moved to New York to pursue a job in medicine. However, without an advanced degree, he couldn't get the jobs he desired. Knowing he had a much-desired skill, Harvey reached out to his friend The Squirrel to put his life saving skills to work. Harvey has become the go-to doctor for the Black criminal underground. On this day, Troy Harvey's surgical skills will be put to the test. The Squirrel helps Lonnie Williams into Harvey's makeshift medical facility outside of Harvey's home on Cruger Avenue in the Bronx.

"Give me the story," asks Harvey as he helps The Squirrel get Williams on the table.

"He was shot three times I believe, but the chest wound is my concern," replies The Squirrel.

Harvey cuts Williams clothes off to assess his wounds.

"These are serious wounds," affirms Harvey as he keeps looking at Williams' injuries.

"Can you save him?" requests a concerned Squirrel.

"I think so. It is going to take some time. Go clean up whatever mess this came from. We will be here," reassures Harvey.

"Thank you, Doc," mentions The Squirrel.

"Whatever this is, watch your back, be careful," offers Harvey as he preps Williams for surgery.

"I gotta make sure Teed is ok," states The Squirrel to himself as he rushes out.

# RESPECT

An unconscious Teed is sitting in a wooden chair bound with a heavy rope in Fritz Kahn's basement. An impatient Luis Sanchez douses Teed with a bucket of cold water to wake him up.

"Dammit!" exclaims an unsuspecting Teed.

"Welcome back," chuckles an amused Sanchez. "What are you doing?" asks Teed.

"That's what I should have asked you," replies Sanchez.

"What?" said Teed.

"You made me lose a bet. He said you would come," jokingly says Sanchez.

"Who said?" requests Teed.

"Kahn, he said you would come for some information. I was like 'no, they gotta know you are ready for them.' Kahn said they are so arrogant they think they are the only smart ones. You made me lose $500 man," claims Sanchez as he shakes his head.

"So now what?" inquires Teed.

"Waiting on a call and then you will die," implies Sanchez.

"This was a plan?" asks Teed.

"Of course, it's a plan. Damn, I had so much respect for you. I heard about all the shit you and Danya Franck pulled off. Some impressive shit if you ask me. Knocked off a president and fucking killed J. Edgar Hoover. Danya Franck sounds like a bad bitch. I could never get my ol' lady to go to the gun range. But you and your group really pissed Kahn off. And he is pretty scary guy," suggests Sanchez.

"Why don't you just get it over with," asks Teed.

"Look, I want to put you out of your misery, but I was told you were to be last. I need to wait until I get the call that Carter and Danya Franck are dead before killing you," answers Sanchez.

Sanchez's words ring in Teed's ears. Teed is not concerned with his own death but the improbable death of his family sends him over the edge. Teed jumps to his feet still bound by the chair.

"You son of a bitch," asserts Teed as he is knocked to the floor by a kick to his stomach by Sanchez causing a loud noise.

"Another $100, he said you would try that dumb shit too," insults Sanchez as he points his gun at Teed.

The phone rings.

"This might be the phone call you don't want," taunts a laughing Sanchez.

Sanchez walks a short five feet away from Teed to answer the phone.

As the phone is ringing, the basement door opens slightly. The Squirrel gets Teed's attention to let him know that he is there. The sight of The Squirrel gives Teed a moment of relief.

"He is tied up. I was waiting for your call. Are both dead?" inquires Sanchez of the caller.

Teed listens intently for the answer.

"Carter, how about Franck? Ok. You want me to handle him now... Ok. I'll do it then clean up. Alright," replies Sanchez as he hangs up the phone.

"Well, change of plans. You actually won't be the last to go. It will be Franck. A delayed flight extends her life for about an extra hour," comments Sanchez as he checks his gaudy gold watch.

The mounting frustration leads Teed to charge Sanchez again.

"Are you serious?" states Sanchez as he points his gun at the charging Teed. The basement door opens wide startling Sanchez. The Squirrel rushes down the stairs firing off two precise shots at Sanchez hitting him in the forehead and dead in his heart. Sanchez is dead before his body hits the floor. Both Teed and Sanchez hit the cold concrete floor at the same time. Their eyes meet, Teed realizes this all could have gone another way as he investigates Sanchez's lifeless eyes as blood streams from his forehead. The Squirrel rushes over to pick Teed up off the floor.

"You alright?" asks The Squirrel as he unties Teed. "We gotta get to Danya and Keleeha. Someone is gonna kill them," says an anxious Teed.

# DESTINATION

Flight number 2204 has arrived from Tehran, Iran into JFK Airport. Wafai Rashad is walking through the airport terminal with a certain pep in his step. The first part of his mission has been a success. Wafai was indifferent to murdering Cecil Thomas. It was a part of Kahn's master plan but the carrot for Wafai Rashad's participation was the eventual murder of Danya Franck. It is the first thought in the morning and his last thought at night how he would exact his revenge on Danya. It has not set well with him that he needed to run from a woman. A very dangerous woman but a woman all the same. A woman that tried to kill him, his Black September brethren and possibly his family. Along his walk, Wafai stops by a bank of lockers. He looks for locker number 324. After finding the locker, Wafai opens it to find a duffle bag full of cash and an envelope. He looks in the envelope discovering a piece of paper with the name Danya Franck and the address of 130 Clay Street Unit F Upper Westside. A devilish smile appears on his face as he closes the locker. Wafai walks out of the terminal to hail a cab. The cab pulls up to him.

"Where ya going?" asks the cabbie.

Wafai looks back at the piece of paper.

"Take me to 130 Clay Street," responds Wafai.

"Upper Westside?" asks the cabbie.

"Yes."

"Hop in."

Wafai jumps in the cab, and they speed off.

On the other side of town, Teed and The Squirrel have run into traffic on the Major Deagan expressway.

"My fucking luck," utters an impatient Teed.

"So, tell me what's going on?" questions The Squirrel.

"Too much, but I gotta get to Danya," declares Teed. He adds, "How was this shit related to what happened at the warehouse?"

The Squirrel answers, "Shit, I hadn't had a chance to tell you. That son of a bitch Rojas' men tried to kill all their drug dealing partners."

"Were you supposed to be there?" inquires a dumbfounded Teed.

"Yeah," said The Squirrel.

"That wasn't meant for the drug dealers, that was meant for you. They were taking all of us out at once," theorizes Teed as the traffic starts to move.

"That killing was for me? I don't know any of those people. That's what I get for following you," remarks The Squirrel as they speed down the expressway.

# THE LAST DANCE

The shiny yellow Checker Cab carrying Wafai Rashad pulls up to 130 Clay Street on the Upper Westside of Manhattan. A slight grin comes over Wafai's face followed by a single tear. On this day, he gets to avenge the deaths of his wife and two of his sons. Wafai has never grieved their deaths. His building vengeance is close to being realized. Wafai exits the vehicle.

"That will be $20," requests the cab driver.

Wafai goes into his pocket and peels off a $100 bill from his bill fold.

"Here you go," offers a thankful Wafai.

"Whoa, do you want change?" inquires the driver.

"Not at all, thank you good sir," recites an appreciative Wafai.

The driver speeds away.

"Let's dance Ms. Franck," remarks Wafai as he walks toward the building.

Danya and Keleeha are enjoying a lazy Sunday evening at home. Teed has been gone since the early morning. Danya is mildly interested in the TV Western "Bonanza" as she plays with Keleeha's curly hair. Keleeha is not interested in Bonanza at all. She has decided to finish reading E.B. White's classic "Charlotte's Web."

"How is the book?" asks Danya.

"It's good," responds Keleeha.

"It has to be better than this awful excuse for a Western," comments Danya as she hears a thud in a back room.

Danya perks up. Her old training kicks in. Danya briskly walks to her bedroom. She looks under her bed for her .22 caliber. In most cases, the .22 caliber wouldn't kill anyone, but it could certainly make a mess. But now Danya is petrified that her gun is missing, and her daughter is not safe. Danya runs back to the living room to find Keleeha still reading Charlotte's Web peacefully. Danya momentarily smiles at Keleeha. In Danya's peripheral vision she notices a man standing in the shadow of the hallway.

"Danya Franck, esteemed Mossad officer or should I say retired Mossad officer," suggests Wafai Rashad.

A startled Keleeha asks Danya,

"Mommy who is that?" Keleeha starts to walk toward Danya.

"Hold on baby, don't...go finish reading your book in your room," begs Danya as Keleeha goes to her room.

"So you are, how do the Americans say?

You are keeping house. You have become an American housewife. You will be the envy of all Israeli women," says a sarcastic Wafai.

"What do want? Are you here to kill me?" demands Danya.

"I am," declares Wafai as he fires a shot at Danya.

Danya is struck in her right leg. She falls to the floor in terrible pain as blood flows from her leg.

"I am going to kill you, but I want you to suffer. Your 8MEN group needed to suffer first. You were my prize. I wanted to kill you earlier," admits Wafai.

"Why didn't you?" asked a pain-riddled Danya.

"I guess it doesn't matter now. My colleague wanted your cohorts to die first then I get to make you suffer," affirms a gleeful Wafai.

"Please leave my daughter alone, please don't hurt her," hopes a begging Danya.

Wafai moves closer to Danya cocking his gun.

"Sorry, no. There will be no witnesses. But I will kill her quick. You have my promise," alleges Wafai.

He aims at Danya. A shot goes off. Danya feels no pain, but she assumes she has been shot. But the shot didn't hit her, it hit Wafai Rashad in the chest. He is in shock as he stumbles back, he is shot in the chest again. Wafai drops the gun as he falls to the floor. Keleeha walks up to Wafai.

"You shot my mommy," speaks Keleeha as she shoots Wafai twice in the head. Moments later Teed and The Squirrel rush in to find Keleeha holding a gun.

"Honey, give daddy the gun," asks Teed.

The Squirrel checks Wafai's lifeless body to make sure he is dead.

Keleeha hands Teed the gun as she gives him a hug.

"Let's check on mommy," suggests a smiling Teed.

Danya is injured but it is not life threatening.

Teed and Keleeha hug Danya tight.

"This is not finished. We need to end this," declares an angry Danya.

"How do you want to do it?" asks Teed.

# LOOSE ENDS

Fritz Kahn has accomplished his goal of destroying the 8MEN and furthering the Lumiere's grip on the world. Kahn's plan was masterful. The 8MEN had made true progress in their pursuit of influencing world events. But like anything, with one gaining power and influence, it threatens the power and influence of others. Kahn and his cronies watched as the 8MEN started their campaign of influence on the American way of life. At the beginning of the 1950's, the group began their global campaign to influence the world. They played a part in destabilizing East Asia, sold military weaponry to both sides of the Middle East conflict, profited off the oil crisis and instigated the destruction of the civil rights movement. The Lumiere co-opting the 8MEN to do its bidding in America was brilliantly done. Not to mention, the sweet revenge that Kahn was about to realize for the assassination of his cousin, J. Edgar Hoover. Kahn walks into his office in a jovial mood. He doesn't see the shadowy figure sitting in the dark.

"You've won," comments the shadowy figure.

"Who?" challenges Kahn.

"Hell of a plan," responds Teed.

"Well thank you. Is that you Teed?" asks Kahn.

Teed turns on a nearby light so that Kahn can see his face and the gun he is holding. Kahn raises his hands showing he is not going to resist.

"I take it, Mr. Rashad has failed?" inquires Kahn.

"He did. Miserably," states Teed.

"So, you are here to end me," utters Kahn as he pours himself a drink.

"I am actually here to get some answers," mentions Teed.

"Since I have nothing but time, ask your questions," responds Kahn.

"Why did you come for us? We didn't do anything to you," asks Teed.

"Of course, you did. You just thought nobody knew. Your cabal was allowed to make money and influence world events because it fell in line with the Lumiere's overall goals. But the murder of Edgar could not be overlooked," admits Kahn.

"So now what do we do? You have killed all the 8MEN," questions Teed.

"I have eliminated all the 8MEN, but I didn't get you and I imagine I didn't get Ms. Franck either. Since we are having a sensible conversation," recites Kahn.

"Sorry to disappoint you but Danya is alive. She is pretty pissed but alive," replies Teed.

"You and Ms. Franck have proven yourselves to be quite cunning. Your group is now gone. Come and work for me and Lumiere. You will be wealthy beyond your imagination. And you will be able to take care of generations of your family," asserts an overly confident Kahn.

"So, you almost kill us, and you scare our daughter, and we are supposed to just let that go?" challenges Teed.

"Your only alternative is to come to work for the Lumiere. What else can you do?" demands Kahn as he is interrupted by the bullet that has pierced his forehead.

"Or we could do that. I told you she was pissed," declares a satisfied Teed.

A steady stream of blood pours from Kahn's forehead as his lifeless body slumps in his chair. Teed walks over to the window and waves to Danya at her sniper's perch at a nearby building.

"I could have forgiven you for coming after me, but my wife couldn't forgive you for coming after our daughter. So, it had to end," states Teed as he talks out of Kahn's office.

# SOLACE

The dream of the 8MEN wielding their influence on America was undoubtedly over. With the deaths of all the group except Valerius Torrantio, Danya and Teed were going to have to find another life path. The death of Wesley Carter was the symbolic end of the 8MEN. The systematic destruction of the cabal was as epic as its meteoric rise. With the only remaining charter member remanded to the country of Italy, it was unlikely the group could ever be reborn. With the stress over the last week, Teed's family needed some well-earned rest and relaxation. Most families would go on vacation or spend a day at an amusement park, but most families don't consist of two of the best spies the world has ever known. Teed and Danya decided to go to the Westchester Gun Club in Rye, New York to teach Keleeha how to use guns properly with confidence. The attempted murder of Danya and Keleeha has brought the budding family even closer together. The escape of the near tragedy has given the family a greater appreciation for each other, but it has also brought the realization that Keleeha needs to be trained in the event any other unsavory characters come calling. Danya and Teed are getting older and Keleeha seems to be a natural. She may be put in a position to protect herself or her parents again. Danya has set up a makeshift sniper's perch to show Keleeha how to position her gun.

"Your target is far away. You can't tell how close or far away your target is without this scope," Danya explains to Keleeha in a motherly tone.

In the distance there are three aluminum cans sitting on a shelf. Keleeha adjusts the dial on the scope to bring the cans into full focus. Feeling confident, Keleeha fires off three shots, hitting all the cans dead center. "Mommy, I hit all three!" shouts Keleeha as she hugs Danya.

Both are excited. A short distance away, a proud Teed watches Keleeha's great progress from a park bench.

"Why can't y'all just go to Playland like regular people," says The Squirrel. The two men embrace.

"You decided to come up?" says Teed.

"Yeah, I thought I would come up and check on y'all. So, what's up?" replies The Squirrel.

"Nothing much. Wanted to say our goodbyes. We are thinking about going back to the Middle East," says Teed.

"Something happen?" asks The Squirrel in a concerned tone. "No," Teed responds. "As crazy as it sounds it's probably safer there." Both men laugh.

"But really there is nothing here for us. I think a change of scenery will be good for Danya and Keleeha," claims Teed with a smile as he looks at both in the distance.

"And for you. Is this going to be good for you?" questions The Squirrel.

"I'm happy any anytime I can see those smiles. This is a good life," states Teed with a giant smile.

FIN

# EPILOGUE

In the early 1980s, the United States Government decided to take a stand against the growing spread of Communism in Central America. The Russian backed Sandinistas were making major strides in Nicaragua and were influencing other governments in the region toward a more socialist ideology.

American president Ronald Reagan campaigned on and later was swept into office on an anti-communist stance that he intended to live up to. The thought of communist nations operating in the Western Hemisphere bothered Reagan to no end.

With communist Cuba still surviving after years of crippling sanctions, Reagan worried that Russia may invest resources in an attempt to destabilize the region. It was believed that if the U.S. had to deal with communism in Central America, then the U.S. wouldn't be able to foster democracy on the Russian doorstep in Eastern Europe. The lessons of the Vietnam War were painful and enlightening all at the same time. After winning World War II in convincing fashion, the American military began to think they could simply win a war because of their military might. But the Vietnam War showed that if American military might was not coupled with a desire for war from the public or the enlisted men, the weapons would be rendered useless.

The Reagan administration knew the American public did not have the appetite for another foreign war, but Reagan felt the U.S. had a duty to stomp out any bastions of communism in the Americas. In order to fight the battle against the Sandinistas, the American Government enlisted the help of a rag-tag group of local fighters that became known as the Contras. The Contras fought a guerrilla style war, they Inflicted damage on the Sandinistas but their destruction also impacted innocent bystanders that had nothing to do with the conflict. The Reagan administration caught flak from Congress about the fighters. Congress put restraints on the monies that could be used for foreign interventions. The Congress withholding funds slated to go the Contras sent Reagan into a rage. He knew the military brass would not go against the spirit of any restraints that congress may have placed on useable funding. But he also knew the CIA didn't have the same philosophical hang ups and would continue to champion the initiative. CIA Director Sean Williams is a 10-year veteran of the clandestine organization. He learned at the feet of Wesley Carter. Carter mentored Williams until his death and viewed him as a father figure. Carter taught him that there were times that you must bend the rules for the greater good. And, Williams felt this was a time to bend the rules. The Sandinistas rule has been bad for local business, legal and illegal. The Sandinistas slowed the free reign of the drug barons of the region. The drug pipeline from South America to the profit centers of Mexico and the United States passed right through Nicaragua. The Rojas drug family has taken a major hit since the Sandinistas takeover. Unlike the prior democratic officials, the Sandinistas weren't so easy to bribe, which has cut the organization's profit by more than half. CIA Director Sean Williams has set a meeting in the bustling Mexican resort town of Cancun with reputed drug lord Micquel Rojas. They set the meeting in Mexico because Rojas is still wanted by the FBI for alleged foreign conspiracy in relation to the death of former CIA Director Wesley Carter.

The men meet at Andeleos, an upscale outdoor restaurant that sits on the beach with limited entourages, not wanting to attract any attention. Micquel Rojas is anxiously waiting for Williams. He knows the Mexican government would never extradite him to the U.S., but you never know what the Americans might have up their sleeves. The comfortably dressed Williams walks over to the awaiting Rojas. Rojas rises to shake Williams' hand.

"Mr. Rojas," says a sterile Williams as he sits without shaking Rojas' hand leaving him stunned. "Mr. Rojas, please let's get something out of the way. I am meeting with you because you are a necessary evil. You are uniquely positioned to help the United States of America. And that is the only reason I am here," barks Williams.

"Why should I help America?" timidly questions Rojas.

Williams grins, "I'm sorry if you felt like I was asking. You are going to help us or we will come for you. We will help you resurrect your business. We will make sure that you are no longer pursued by American law enforcement. In exchange for you getting your business back, you will serve as benefactor to the Contras in Nicaragua. Do I make myself clear?" questions Williams.

"Crystal," responds Rojas.

Williams answers, "This should be a great partnership, or not."

# APPRECIATION

To those that have helped and inspired me. 8MEN would not have been possible without you. Your words, your kindness and your tough love made a difference. I am eternally thankful to you.

John & Bernell Smith, Pamela Love, Sean Smith, Sierra Smith, Terry Watkins, Bryant & Rachel Watkins, Kevin and Kelsey Allen, Addie B. Johnson, Florence Smith, Romaine Parker, Tonya Love, Christal Gaston, Nana Afrieye, Dr. Nana Kokoroko, William & Patricia Love, John & Blanche Harris, Melvin & Nancy Parker, Scott & Craig Carrington , Richard & Meka Parker, Aaron Harris, John I. Harris III., Che Grillo, Julian Williams, Shelly Davis, Bryanna Caleb, C Dian & Kevin Carter, Jason & Frankie Carter, Elaine & Loren, Carter, Andre & Kristie Harvey, Chauka Reid, Brenda & Doug Leake, Victoria & Gary Person, Stacy & Guy Polk, Steve & Erica Bates, Andre' & Anthony Savoy, Al & Paul Green, Reggie "Reckless" Coleman, Kenneth "Black" Riley, Camille Thomas, Cecily Bush, Michael Grisby, Shannon Day, Terrae Brown, LaChelle Hyman, Germaine Smith, Patricia Taylor, Rae Swann, Ricardo Fox, Larry Beavers, Flo Ann Taylor, Tina Moreland, Meico Green, Ramona Simms, Jeanette Davis, Trisha Quarles, Marcy Allsup, Ayanna Green-Harris, Zanette Burrell, Stacey King, Tracy McKinney, Ramsay Johnson, Teresa Bradshaw, Raymond & Margaret Steadman, Raymond

Steadman, Jr. Carol Fox, Mary, Hernandez, Diane, & Ed Gadsden, Monica Brown, Luis & Stephanie Grillo, Micha & Donnie Harris, Norman Parker, Tim Massey, Stephen Banian, Tracy Miles, Theodore Hicks, Randy Banks, Robert Monk , Monique Richardson, Eugene Rudder, Andel Owens, Johnny Garnett, Jeff Flournoy, Keenon James, Mike Williams, Lonnie Stancil, George Parson, Otis Adkins, Charles Twitty, Greg Robinson, Floyd DeWitt, Jason Hill, Daryl and Lisa Watson, The Brothers of the "U", Darrin Carter, Dave Felton, Trevor Morris, Malika Carey, Anthony Johnson, Jr. Brown Family (Charleston SC), Kevin Thompson, Angela Johnson, Chris White, Grace Morris, Guy Coates, Dana Lyons, Denise Wilkerson, Harold and Michelle Scott, Marjorie & Walter Winston, Malcolm & Lauren Augustine, Kara Penn, Carol Vance, Carl Barnes, Glenard Moulden, Rhonda Stenson, Paula Sparrow, Evelyn & Curtis Bennett, Tara Shea-Newsome,  St. Mary's family (Annapolis) , SAS family, Bay Boyz, 4th Ward family, Sheik Njie, Michael Crutchfield.

Thank you all

In an Era of booming patriotism following the end of World War II, a secret society manipulates the destiny of America. The 8MEN organization borrows leadership from the nation's biggest industries--oil, media, the CIA...even the mafia.

Ricky Teed, an idealistic soldier and spy, travels the world on missions for the 8MEN.

But as the domestic operations grow increasingly sinister, Teed begins to spiral, questioning his values, morality, patriotism...when did preserving the American way turn into a web of lies and murder?